An Undeniable Secret

AMISH SECRETS
~ BOOK 4 ~

J. E. B. Spredemann

Blessed Publishing

Published in Indiana by Blessed Publishing.

www.jebspredemann.com

Cover design by J.E.B. Spredemann

BOOKS BY J.E.B. SPREDEMANN
(*J. Spredemann)

AMISH GIRLS SERIES

Joanna's Struggle

Danika's Journey

Chloe's Revelation

Susanna's Surprise

Annie's Decision

Abigail's Triumph

Brooke's Quest

Leah's Legacy

NOVELLAS*

Amish by Accident*

An Unforgivable Secret* - Amish Secrets 1

A Secret Encounter* - Amish Secrets 2

A Secret of the Heart* - Amish Secrets 3

An Undeniable Secret* - Amish Secrets 4

Learning to Love – Saul's Story* (Sequel to Chloe's Revelation – adult novella)

A Christmas of Mercy – Amish Girls Holiday

For my daddy…
you'll always be my hero

Author's Note

It should be noted that the Amish people and their communities differ one from another. There are, in fact, no two Amish communities exactly alike. It is this premise on which this book is written. We have taken cautious steps to assure the authenticity of Amish practices and customs. Both Old Order Amish and New Order Amish are portrayed in this work of fiction and may be inconsistent with some Amish communities.

We, as *Englischers*, can learn a lot from the Plain People and their simple way of life. Their hard work, close-knit family life, and concern for others are to be applauded. As the Lord wills, may this special culture continue to be respected and remain so for many centuries to come, and may the light of God's salvation reach their hearts.

Characters in
An Undeniable Secret

The Troyer Family

Elam – Saloma's father

Rosemary – Saloma's mother

Saloma aka Sally – oldest daughter, Protagonist

Clara, Lucinda, Rosy, Mary, Katy, Judy, Becky – Saloma's sisters

The Griffith Family

Peter – William's father

Sandra – William's mother

William aka Will – Protagonist

Others

George Anderson aka Uncle George – William's uncle

Elam Zook – resident of Kentucky Amish district

Pastor Rob – William's pastor

Jonathan Fisher – Amish minister and popular character woven throughout all of J.E.B. Spredemann's books thus far, most notably the Amish Girls Series

Unofficial Glossary
of Pennsylvania Dutch Words

Ach – Oh

Aldi – Girlfriend

Boppli – Baby

Bopplin – Babies

Dat – Dad

Denki – Thanks

Der Herr – The Lord

Dochder – Daughter

Englischer – A non-Amish person

Fraa – Woman, Wife

Gott – God

Gut – Good

Jah – Yes

Kinner – Children

Mamm – Mom

Nee – No

Ordnung – Rules of the Amish Community

Vadder – Father

Wilkom – Welcome

PROLOGUE

*S*aloma glanced at the clock on the wall for the fourth time in the last ten minutes. What was taking *Mamm* and *Dat* so long? They should have been home over an hour ago. Perhaps they'd been held up by traffic. *Jah*, that was it. She was sure of it.

Nobody had been expecting *Dat* to fall out of his chair this morning. Not her, not *Mamm*, and certainly not *Dat* himself. Saloma and *Mamm* had been in the kitchen, preparing scrapple and eggs for breakfast, when they heard a loud thump on the hardwood floor. Both of the women rushed into the living room the moment they'd heard the noise, knowing that *Dat* wouldn't have allowed the *kinner* to horseplay inside. There had to be something wrong.

Unfortunately, their instincts had been correct. Saloma attempted to fathom the scene playing out before her eyes. *Dat* lay on the floor helpless, like a brand new kid wrapped in its mother's sac, waiting to be rescued from impending death. He clenched his arm and his disillusioned eyes met *Mamm's*. Saloma recognized fear in *Dat's* solemn gaze, something she'd never experienced in all her growing up years. *Dat* had always been strong and confident – a leader of his meager tribe of eight *maed*. *Dat* had never been blessed with sons, and Saloma often wondered whether he regretted that fact. Had tending the farm alone been too much of a burden for him?

Another five minutes passed and still no word from *Mamm*. Was *Dat* still breathing, or had he passed on to Glory? Sometimes, the unknown almost seemed worse than the actual knowing of a matter. If *Dat* were to pass on, she'd be the one *Mamm* would rely on for strength, but she was unsure she could provide it. Her own heart would need mending if she were to be of help to anybody.

But she wouldn't think of that now. No, *Dat* was still alive. He had to be.

Pray. Pray hard.

ONE

Grieving the Loss of a Loved One, Saloma read the spine of the library book and pulled it from its position on the shelf. It seemed she needed all the help she could get in dealing with the loss of her father. The younger *kinner* would certainly be asking more questions as the days passed, and she wanted to be able to give sufficient answers and support. She added it to the pile beside her on the floor.

"That's a good book."

Saloma startled at the male voice and spun around. She was unprepared for the handsome *Englischer* who stood just inches before her. She unconsciously touched her prayer *kapp*. "Do you usually sneak up on Amish women in libraries?" She couldn't help the words that flew from her mouth unbridled, a fault she hoped to one day overcome.

"Actually, I do." The man chuckled. "No, not really. Just kidding."

"Oh, sorry. I just, uh, sometimes I say things." She flustered.

"Well, I'd say that's good. You know, some people don't have the ability to speak." He winked.

"Stupid things, I mean."

He smiled and held out his hand. "My name's William. Will, for short."

"*Gut* to meet you, Will." She shook his hand briefly, and then scanned the area for a nearby empty table. "I was going to find a place to sit down now."

"Okay. Would you mind if I join you?"

What does this Englischer *want?* "Uh, *jah*, I guess that would be okay." She bent down to pick up the books.

"Here, let me get those."

"*Denki.*"

"You didn't tell me your name. Or did your mother teach you not to talk to library-stalking strangers?"

Saloma cracked a half-smile. This *Englischer* was certainly different than anyone she'd met. "No, my mother did not say that. I've spoken to many strangers." She led the way to a table that had two comfy-looking chairs across from one another.

William chuckled and followed her to the quiet corner nook.

"Why is that funny?" Saloma watched as Will set the stack of books on the table. This *Englischer* was more handsome than any of the Amish men her age, hands down. She found his short dark hair attractive, she admitted. However, he was *Englisch,* and that meant out of her league. Nevertheless, she enjoyed this *Englischer's* attention.

"Not funny. Cute."

Saloma's cheeks flamed. "I don't understand."

"You *still* haven't told me your name." He raised a brow.

"Saloma."

"A nice name, but it reminds me of salami." He chuckled again, his hazel eyes sparkling. "Saloma. Saloma." The name rolled off his tongue. "Would you be offended if I called you Sally? That's much easier for me to remember. Besides, I think you look more like a Sally than a Saloma."

"Sally?" She thought for a moment then shrugged. "*Jah*, I reckon that would be okay." It's not like she would ever see this *Englischer* again.

He pulled the top book off the stack. His gaze turned solemn. "This book really helped me after my father passed away last year. He was a great man, and I took his death pretty hard."

"Your *vatter* died too?"

Will nodded.

"My *va-*father died last week." Tears immediately filled Saloma's eyes unbidden.

Will reached over and squeezed her fingers briefly, then released her hand. "I'm so sorry."

She pulled a handkerchief from her dress sleeve and dabbed her eyes.

"I know it's probably really difficult right now, but you'll get through it. God will help you."

Saloma nodded. "It was His will, *jah*."

"Tell me about your father. What sort of man was he?"

"He was a *gut,* kind man. He worked hard." She thought about her father and the countless hours he'd spent farming so they'd have plenty to eat, or cutting wood to provide warmth during the winter months. A son would have been an immense help, but the Lord had never blessed her folks with male offspring. "There are eight of us *kinner* and *Mamm.*"

"My parents had me and my brother, but Christopher died as a baby. So, I basically grew up as an only child."

"It is just your *mamm* and you now?"

"No, my mother died about five years ago."

Saloma frowned. "So, you have nobody?"

"I have God." Will smiled. "And an aunt who lives in Arizona or somewhere out West. I've never met her."

"You live all by yourself then?"

"No, I do have an uncle too. He's my mother's brother. I live with him but he's really busy, so it's almost like I live by myself." He shrugged. "I don't mind, though. I have a lot of freedom."

Saloma placed a hand over her rumbling stomach. "Goodness, it must be near dinner time already."

"I'm getting hungry too." Will smiled and glanced at his watch. "It's actually past lunch time. One-fifteen. Would you like to go grab a bite to eat?"

"I have to be back to pick the *kinner* up from school."

"How long do you have?"

"I should leave in twenty minutes."

6

"I'll tell you what; leave your buggy here and we can take my Jeep. We can just get a pretzel at the pretzel factory. It shouldn't take long." He quirked a brow. "How does that sound?"

Saloma thought of the cash in her wallet. Five dollars should be enough. "*Gut.*"

"Great." He glanced at her pile of books. "Do you need to check those books out?"

"*Jah.*" She gathered her books and Will scooped them into his capable arms.

"Okay, let's go." He grinned.

William pulled off a piece of the soft pretzel in his hand then glanced at the beautiful young woman across the table from him. "You know, Sally, you're the first Amish woman I've actually met."

Saloma's head tilted and her charming smile brightened her face. "I hope you're not disappointed."

"On the contrary; I'm pleasantly surprised." He popped the warm, buttery bread into his mouth.

"Surprised?" Her sapphire eyes sparkled.

"I guess most of the Amish women I've seen don't seem to be too friendly."

"It's not our way to be friendly with male strangers."

"And yet you are." He smiled. "I must be special."

"Ignoring you would have been rude."

"Indeed." He glanced at his watch. "We don't have much time. Let's go."

She nodded and followed him to his Jeep.

After assisting Sally, he hopped in and turned the engine over. "May I see you again, Sally?"

A becoming blush darkened her fair cheeks. "I don't know. This is not normal for Amish. My mother wouldn't approve."

His confidence deflated and he briefly glanced at his plaid shirt. He couldn't pinpoint exactly what it was, but he felt like he'd connected with Sally on a deeper level. She was a pretty girl and he was physically attracted to her, that was true, but there was just something about her that made him desire to know her better. Could he just walk away and forget about her? He didn't think so. Surely there was a way to see her again. "Might you visit the library again soon?"

"I usually come on Tuesdays, after morning chores are done."

Perfect. He smiled. "I just might have to come back to the library next Tuesday, then. Would you mind?"

"It's a free country." She shrugged nonchalantly, but he didn't buy it one bit. Her body language clearly demonstrated her attraction to him as well.

"And isn't that a blessing?" He winked, and she quickly looked away. Yes, she was attracted to him but she seemed to fight it. He didn't know much about the Amish at all, although he'd lived in Lancaster County his entire life. She'd said her mother wouldn't approve. Did that mean that she wasn't allowed to date a non-Amish person? He'd have to do some online research as soon as he got home. He'd never had much interest in the Amish, but now that's all he could think about.

"Here we are." His black Jeep rolled to a stop just next to her buggy. He snatched her books before she had the chance, and carried them to her buggy.

"Thank you for the pretzel." She moved to unhitch the horse, then hopped up onto the bench seat.

"It was my pleasure. Really." He smiled. "I hope you had a good time."

She bit her bottom lip and nodded.

"Me too. See you on Tuesday." William waved as she set off out of the parking lot and down the road. Next Tuesday couldn't come soon enough.

As Saloma approached home, her hands began to tremble. Would *Mamm* know she'd been with an *Englisch* man? Was it written on her face? Would *Mamm* be able to see it in her eyes? Saloma realized that she was on dangerous ground. How could she be so attracted to this *Englischer*? He was indisputably *verboten*. And undeniably desirable.

God, help me.

TWO

"Mr. Griffith, will you be taking your supper with your uncle this evening?"

William glanced at his laptop screen, and turned to the housekeeper. "Yes, Marita, thank you; tell my uncle I'll be there in just a minute."

"Very well, sir." The petite, middle-aged Hispanic woman disappeared from the room.

William turned back to his laptop, and quickly bookmarked the web page so he could return to it later. He never knew the Amish culture could be so fascinating...and perplexing. How could some Amish only own buggies, but hire *Englisch* drivers to take them places? And yet others owned vehicles, but could not drive them? Then, other, more progressive groups owned and drove vehicles? And then there was all different manner of what was acceptable in dress. Why did they call non-Amish people *'Englisch'*? And why is it that some groups did not allow modern conveniences of any kind – not even indoor plumbing, he'd discovered to his dismay – yet others had kitchens and bathrooms that rivaled almost any *Englisch* person's home? Perplexing, indeed.

"Ah, I wondered whether you'd ever pull yourself away from your computer," his uncle commented as he entered the dining room.

"Sorry, Uncle George."

"What has you so thoroughly captivated this evening?" His uncle's curiosity was piqued.

"The Amish." Will smiled.

His uncle frowned. "Why are you concerned with the Amish all of a sudden?"

"I find them interesting, I guess." His uncle didn't need to know anything about his afternoon with Sally.

"Interesting? They're hardly that. Nothing but trouble if you ask me." He scowled.

Why did it seem his uncle had an aversion to the Amish? "Why do you say that, Uncle George? I thought they were known as honest, hard-working people."

"Honest?" he scoffed. "Not the ones I've known."

"But you can't judg–"

"William! Enough of this conversation." His uncle took the cloth napkin before him and placed it over his lap. "Let's discuss something pleasant over our meal, shall we?"

Will sighed. "As you wish, Uncle George." He silently bowed his head to pray.

"How are your studies coming along?"

"Fine. I can't wait to graduate this semester."

"Do you have any job prospects?"

"I haven't looked yet. I've been pouring all of my time into my studies. I thought I'd begin looking as soon as I graduate."

"I heard Grace Chapel has an opening for a youth minister."

He'd considered that position, but it wasn't what he'd had in mind. "I'd hoped to get a counseling position. At a smaller church," he added. Large crowds frightened him. One-on-one counseling seemed to suit his personality best.

"Something like that wouldn't pay much." His uncle's brow lowered. "You do realize that, don't you?"

"I know." He often thought about how he'd be able to support a family if God ever blessed him with one of his own.

"I hope you're not planning to live off your father's meager life insurance policy your whole life. And I refuse to support you indefinitely. I promised your father that I'd see that you completed your college courses; after that, you're on your own."

William glanced around, taking in the opulence of his uncle's large estate. He could easily support ten families if he had a mind to. "I have no intentions of burdening you with my presence," he spat out bitterly.

"William, that's not what I meant."

"Really? Because that was how it sounded." He grimaced. "I'm thankful that you took me in after my father passed away. I plan to have a family of my own someday but, since I have *no one* in my life right now, I'd thought maybe you could fill that void. I guess I was wrong."

He abruptly rose from his chair and left the table. *Is that all I am to Uncle George, just a financial burden?* A dull ache clenched his heart. He missed his parents' love now more than ever.

"Saloma?" She jumped. It seemed like she'd been in a trance half the night, her mind inundated with thoughts of the handsome young *Englisch* man.

She acknowledged John Glick's presence.

"May I drive you home tonight?" He nervously fidgeted with his straw hat.

As long as she could remember, John had been attracted to her. He was *gut*-looking enough, and friendly too, but she hadn't joined the church yet. She didn't think that she wouldn't someday, but something held her back. At present, it was the *Englischer*.

John stood waiting for her answer. "Do you have someone else in mind to ride with?" He glanced around the room.

"*Ach, nee.* I, uh," she couldn't find a good excuse, "okay, John, I'll ride with you."

"Okay, *gut*. I'll hitch up the horse."

Fern Mast sidled up to her as soon as John disappeared. "Are you gonna be ridin' home with John tonight?" Saloma didn't miss the excitement in her friend's voice.

Saloma nodded demurely.

Fern beamed. "I'd hoped you two would get together. He's perfect for you, *ain't so?*"

"Only *Der Herr* knows who's perfect for me," Saloma reminded.

"Maybe so, but I bet it's John Glick."

"I better go. I think I just saw his buggy pull up."

Saloma did her best to think of something other than her father's death, or Will, but it seemed like she'd thought of little else the last few days.

"I'm sorry about what happened with your *daed*. He was a *gut* man."

Saloma raised a half smile at John. "*Jah*, he was."

"What will your *mamm* do now? With the farm and all?"

She and her mother had been discussing that very thing. What they really needed was a man to oversee the farm. "We're unsure yet."

"I could help."

"*Denki*, John. I appreciate that. I'll let my mother know."

He nodded. "You know, it may be too soon, but I'm thinking that, if the two of us get hitched, I could run the farm."

Saloma's jaw dropped. *Did he really just propose what I think he did?*

"I mean, if you'll agree to it."

"John, I'm not even baptized yet. And I don't think I'm ready to marry."

"I see." Lines of disappointment creased his face.

"My father just passed away, and I need some time. We have to adjust."

"I know. I was just thinkin', that's all. Beings y'all don't have a man around."

Saloma knew he only meant the best. "It's a kind offer, John. *Denki* for thinking of us."

"I do like you a whole lot, Saloma. I wouldn't just be marrying ya for the farm."

"I realize that, John. It's a *gut* offer."

"Will ya think on it then?"

"*Jah.* I'll think about it."

John leaned over and kissed her cheek. "*Denki*, Saloma. I will make a *gut* husband for you if ya say yes."

"I'm sure you would, John."

THREE

Saloma rushed to finish up the *kinner's* lunches so they wouldn't be late for school this morning. She turned to the girls. "Mary, Katy, Judy, Becky, do you have your sweaters?"

"*Jah*," the girls replied in unison.

Saloma watched out the window as the girls hopped onto their scooters and made their way toward the schoolhouse down the road. It seemed like only yesterday that she and her other sisters, who were all now finished with their parochial schooling, had been the ones walking or riding their scooters to school. In the colder months, they'd use a buggy or a homemade sleigh *Dat* had made.

Oh, how she missed her *vatter*. He hadn't been perfect by any means, but she knew for certain sure that he was better than a lot of her friends' fathers. *Dat* always took good care of his family, and showed his love for them in many ways. While many Amish fathers didn't show affection, *Dat* had always been sure to compliment the *kinner* when they did well, with at least a pat on the back.

She wondered now what *Dat* would say about Will. It seemed to Saloma that *Der Herr* had orchestrated their meeting at the library. Why else would he place the two of them there at the same time? Why else had William read the very same book she'd decided to check out? There were simply too many coincidences for her to believe that God didn't somehow have a hand in this.

Saloma shook her head to dispel her daydreaming. Now that the girls were taken care of, she could finish up the shopping list and then head into town. Her first stop would be the grocery store, then she'd visit the library for a while. The groceries should keep until her time at the library was up, although she hated to think about her time with Will ending before it had even begun.

As she manuvered the buggy onto the road, she wondered what she would say to William. How much could she possibly have in common with an *Englischer,* anyway? Judging by the last time they met, they had plenty in common. Would he ask her to join him for a pretzel again?

Wait, she was getting ahead of herself. There was a possibility that he wouldn't even be there. What if something came up? What if he changed his mind, and he really wasn't interested at all? What if she read too much into their conversation last time?

All she knew is that she'd better calm her nerves before she arrived at the library. The last thing she needed was to be so nervous that she got tongue-tied. *That* would be embarrassing.

Saloma took a deep breath and glanced over her list one last time, to make sure she'd purchased everything. She had.

Time to head to the library.

William glanced into his rearview mirror to make sure he didn't have anything stuck between his teeth. *Nope.* He looked at his hair. *Fine.*

He usually wasn't this nervous when seeing a girl. For some reason, though, he had a feeling about Sally. She wasn't just another girl. She was different.

A horse's clip-clop drew his attention to the approaching buggy. It was her. He fiddled with his collar, and tried desperately not to stare in her direction. As soon as she neared the hitching post, he hopped out of his Jeep.

"There she is." His face brightened.

He watched as she tethered the horse to the hitching post. Were her hands shaking?

"Hello, Will."

"Did you get a chance to read through that stack of books?" He noticed that she only brought a few back with her.

"*Jah.* I read a couple of them."

"How long do you plan to be here?" He hoped that she didn't have to rush off again, like last time. He had plans.

"The girls took their scooters to school today, so I won't have to pick them up. But I do have groceries in the buggy."

He glanced at the buggy and noticed a large ice chest. "Would you like to go for a drive? I think your groceries should be fine."

Her eyebrows shot up. "Where?"

He shrugged. "Just around. I thought I'd show you where I live, and maybe we could have lunch."

Sally nodded. "That sounds *gut*. I want to return these books first. I'm not planning to borrow any this time. I still have plenty to read."

"Okay. I'll wait for you, Sally." William cracked his knuckles as he watched her walk toward the library book-drop. As soon as she returned, he gallantly opened the door for her.

"Do you live nearby?"

"Not too far from here."

"Your uncle's house, right?"

"You remembered." He nodded, but grimaced inwardly. What would Uncle George say if he knew he was bringing an Amish girl into his home? Fortunately, Uncle George was working at his office in the city today. "I think you'll like it."

"Do you farm?"

"Farm?" He chuckled. "No, I don't know the first thing about farming. Do you?"

"*Jah*. We have corn."

"I've shucked corn before. Does that count?"

Sally smiled and shook her head. "No, but it may come in handy when it's time for canning."

"Are you planning to put me to work already?" He caught her eye as he turned onto his uncle's lane.

She laughed and bit her bottom lip. "Maybe."

"I'll have to remember that."

"This is your uncle's place? It looks very fancy." Her eyes grew large as she took in the splendor, of which his uncle had an abundance.

"Yes, it is. I've had to get used to it. My folks' place wasn't nearly this extravagant. My father was a preacher, so we didn't have a whole lot of money. Our home was quite modest in comparison."

"My *dat* worked on our farm."

"How many acres do you have?" He pulled up to the large circular drive and brought the vehicle to a stop.

"Only eighty."

"Sounds like a nice piece of land. Will one of your brothers farm it, then?" He remembered reading that most Amish had an abundance of children, usually seven or more. Some even had seventeen.

"I have no brothers."

He turned to face her. "So, what will you do?"

She sighed. "We don't know yet."

Will reached over and grasped her fingers. "God will see that it all works out."

21

Sally nodded and stared at their fingers.

"Come on, let me show you my uncle's place." He smiled.

Saloma could hardly believe Will lived in such a fancy home. Everything was immaculate and gorgeous, from the shrubs lining the long driveway to the colorful flower garden that sat in the midst of the circular drive.

"What do you think, Sally?"

Sally. She loved the way her name sounded coming from Will's lips. At first, the nickname seemed strange, but she'd quickly come to adore Will's special name for her.

She glanced down at their intertwined hands. "It's lovely."

He smiled. "As are you." Will reached into a rose bush, plucked off a flower, and handed it to her.

Saloma's cheeks flamed once again. Could Will be any more perfect for her? Well, *jah*, he could be Amish.

He pulled open one of the large intricately-carved doors and they stepped into an expansive foyer. She looked up at the elaborate chandelier that projected a rainbow of colors on the floor and walls. "Oh, William, it's beautiful! I've never seen anything like it. *Ach*, I imagine this is what Heaven will be like."

"No, I'm quite certain Heaven will be much better than this." He chuckled and took her by the hand as they entered another room.

A small Hispanic woman with graying hair stepped into the room as well. "Mr. Griffith, your lunch will be ready in about five minutes."

"Thank you, Marita. Would you mind fixing it up in a picnic basket for us? The lady and I will take our lunch outdoors."

"Certainly, sir." She nodded, and cast a curious smile in Saloma's direction. "I will leave it on the table for you. Will you be needing a blanket as well?"

"Yes, please. I appreciate that."

Saloma watched as the lady disappeared into another room, which she assumed to be the kitchen. "Is she your cook?"

"Marita does a lot of things for us. Meal preparation is just one of her duties. She's been employed by my uncle for many years."

"She seems like a nice person."

William's perplexing gaze transformed into a full-fledged smile. "You're something else."

"I don't know what you mean."

"You seem to find beauty in everything."

"There is beauty in everything. Sometimes you just have to look a little harder, because it is hidden…like a buried treasure."

"You're amazing, Sally." His eyes met hers, and she noticed something in their depths. Desire.

Surely her cheeks were ablaze with color. "*Denki.*"

"Come now; let me show you my favorite place in the house." William led the way down a long hall, passing several doors until they came to the entrance of another room. "Close your eyes."

She did as told, and briefly thought that he might kiss her. Instead, to a small degree of disappointment, he led her by the hand.

"You may open your eyes now."

Her disappointment was quickly replaced with awe as she gazed upon shelf after shelf of beautiful books on every wall. The room wasn't too large, only twice the size of her bedroom, but the grandeur was breathtaking. "What is this place?"

"It's my uncle's library. Do you like it?"

She slowly walked along the walls, reading the titles of the books. A comfortable oversized couch beckoned her to curl up in its cushions with a novel. She could only imagine how cozy the room was in the dead of winter, with the rock fireplace lit. "It's splendid!"

"Maybe we can spend more time here another day."

The thought of spending more time with Will thrilled her heart. This all seemed like a pleasant dream. Was she really here? "That would be wonderful."

"Right now, lunch awaits."

In one hand, William carried the picnic basket with the quilt draped over it. He purposely kept his other one free so he could walk hand-in-hand with Sally. He found a shady spot under one of the magnificent oaks in the yard. The two of them spread out the quilt and plopped down onto it. Sally was beautiful inside and out; it took every ounce of restraint to not kiss her.

He peered into the picnic basket and smiled: macaroni salad, carrot sticks, chicken salad sandwiches, and cookies for dessert. Marita had done a fine job preparing lunch for them, Will acknowledged. He'd have to thank her again later.

He handed a plastic plate to Sally, some utensils, and a sandwich, and her face brightened. He loved to see her excitement at even the smallest of luxuries.

"We don't ever make this kind of bread, but I've seen it before. What is it called?"

"These are croissants."

She took a bite before he could offer a prayer. "They are delicious."

William wouldn't voice the thought that automatically popped into his head at her comment. He shook his head in an attempt to dissuade the improper thought. "Yes, I like them too. Do you mind if I pray?" Yes, he should definitely pray. Now.

"That is fine."

He bowed his head, but peeked to see how she would respond. Her head briefly rose when he began praying aloud. He'd read that the Amish usually pray silently over their meals, and wondered now if it seemed strange to hear him pray aloud.

A thought crossed his mind. Since it was usually the man, the head of the house, who prayed in an Amish home, who said the blessing at Sally's family table now that her father was gone?

He didn't want to spoil this moment with a gloomy subject, so he didn't voice his question. He'd have to research it later.

"Would you like some carrots and macaroni salad? Marita made plenty," he offered.

"*Jah. Denki.*"

Sally surveyed the yard. "*Ach,* I didn't know you had a swing!"

Will smiled as he remembered times past. The swing, with its long ropes, always made him feel as though he were soaring through the sky, like an eagle on the wind. "Yep."

She sprung from her place on the quilt and charged toward the swing. William ran after her, but she reached it first and plopped down onto the seat.

"I've got to warn you, this thing goes really high."

"Will you push me?" The excitement in her voice couldn't be tampered.

Will nodded and came behind her. His heart quickened its beat as he stood close, his hands on the ropes beside her. He pulled the ropes back and whispered in her ear, "Are you ready?"

She nodded and he pulled back a little more.

"Higher," she urged.

He stepped back even further until the swing reached the height of his chest. "Hang on." Will let go of the ropes and watched with delight as Sally flew through the air. He still remembered the thrill he experienced when his father let go of his first push.

"Wee!"

Will smiled at her enthusiasm. He'd never seen an adult this excited about swinging. "How long has it been since you've swung?"

"Not since school. Five years ago."

He frowned. "How old are you?" He supposed he should have asked that question already.

"Nineteen. How old are you?"

"Twenty-three." He waited until she brought the swing to a stop. "Done already?" His brow rose.

"Don't you want to?"

He stood in front of her and met her gaze. "Yes, I want to." However, he wouldn't without her permission.

The meaning of his words registered in her eyes. She nodded oh so briefly. That was all the consent he needed.

Without breaking eye-contact, he lowered his lips onto hers. When she closed her eyes, he did as well. If this was her first kiss, he never would have known it. Her hands cradled his neck, and she deepened the kiss.

If he had any doubt about her feelings toward him – or his for her – it fled the moment their lips met. He eventually broke contact, desperate for reprieve.

"Sorry." She bit her lip.

His breathing came hard. "Oh, no. Don't be sorry. I just broke away because...well, you know." He caressed her face. "Man, that was wonderful!"

"I thought so too."

He glanced back toward their picnic blanket, lest their lips meet again. "Should we finish our lunch?"

She smiled. "*Jah*. We'd better."

FOUR

*W*illiam turned the page and scribbled furiously in his notebook. By the look of it, one would think he was cramming for a final. But that couldn't be further from reality. He determined to read every piece of literature he could get his hands on, regarding the Amish and their culture.

One thing he'd learned was that they seemed to be walking contradictions regarding a lot of things. And Sally – Saloma – proved his point. It was absolutely clear that she cared for him, but she seemed reticent somehow. No, not with her kisses – she gave those quite freely. He observed that she only allowed herself to feel and experience in part, emotionally-speaking.

When he'd mentioned a relationship, and alluded to a possible future together, she seemed apprehensive. For the life of him, he couldn't figure out the problem. Was she afraid to get too close?

He sat in front of his laptop again, but this time he typed in 'Amish dating and marriage'. His eyes roamed over a foreign word: *rumspringa*. He'd heard the term before, but had never learned its meaning. '*Rumspringa* literally means running around. It's a period of time, recognized by some Amish communities, for young people (usually between the ages of sixteen and early twenties) to seek a mate and taste a little bit of the *Englisch* world. Some Amish young folks will drive cars, drink alcohol, and even date non-Amish, whom they call *Englischers.* The majority of Amish young folks decide to stay within their familiar communities, but some do leave to embrace an *Englisch* lifestyle. The Amish have an eighty-five percent retention rate.' *Wow, eighty-five percent!* William read that last line again to be sure he'd read it correctly.

"I see you're hard at work again." Uncle George walked into the library. "Do you have exams approaching?"

"No, they're still a couple months away."

"What are you working on now?"

"Research." William briefly glanced at his uncle, and then turned back to the screen.

"That's vague."

"Last time I told you what I was researching you got bent out of shape."

The heavy sigh from his uncle was not unexpected. "What is this fascination you have with the Amish?"

"I'm dating an Amish girl."

Silence.

William tried to determine what Uncle George would say next. He suspected his response to this new revelation wouldn't be positive.

"That's not a good idea," his uncle finally spoke.

William's jaw clenched. "I think it's a great idea."

"You should read *that* book." He pointed to the Bible beside William. "It'll give you a little wisdom. Read the part about not being unequally yoked."

"Since when do *you* care about what the Bible says? You haven't stepped foot in a church in years, Uncle George."

"We're not discussing *my* life."

"Who I date is none of your business."

"That's where you're wrong, William. You are my sister's son. Since neither she nor your father is here anymore, I have a responsibility for you."

"I'm not a child anymore."

"Perhaps not in age, but your poor choices indicate that you lack the maturity to make adult decisions."

"Are you serious?" William raked his hand through his hair. "You want to dictate who I go out with?" He stood up and leveled his gaze at his uncle. "No."

"William, I feel that your parents would have agreed with me on this."

William's fist clenched and he felt his fingernails digging into his palm. *How dare he presume to know what Mom and Dad would think!* He took a deep breath in an effort to respond calmly. "I respectfully disagree with you. I *know* my parents would love Sally."

"There are millions of women out there who *aren't* Amish. You can find someone else."

31

"Why are you so prejudiced against them? You've never even met Sally."

"I have my reasons."

"Well, I'm sorry you feel that way, but I don't. I've never met *anyone* like Sally before, and I'm pretty sure that she's the one God wants me to marry. If you can't handle that, then I don't know what to say to you. As far as I'm concerned, we have nothing more to discuss."

William scooped his laptop into his arms and fled the room.

Saloma whistled as she sent the clothing piece-by-piece through the wringer washer. When *Dat* added the laundry room to the house, it had been a huge blessing. She no longer had to carry the laundry up and down the basement stairs, which had been a difficult task when the clothes were heavy with dampness.

As she hung the laundry on the line, thoughts of her time with Will filled her head. *Ach*, he was certainly the kindest man she'd ever known. And he was ever so handsome. What would a life with Will be like? An *Englisch* life would be so different than what she'd always known.

She glanced at the laundry lightly blowing in the breeze. Most *Englisch* folks didn't even use a clothes line, did they? She looked down at her plain dress, with her cape and apron. If she were *Englisch*, what would she wear? Would she don men's trousers like most of the *Englisch* women she'd seen, or would she wear a pretty, colorful dress? What would William want her to wear?

The clip-clop of an approaching horse made her think of Will's transportation. Could she learn to drive an automobile like the *Englisch*? How would she go about getting her driver's license? Where would she attend meeting? Would she have to go out and get a job or would William want her to stay home? Did Will believe that children were a gift from God, and would he want to have as many as God blessed them with, or would he only want one or two like some *Englisch* families had?

All these foreign thoughts made her dizzy. For certain, if she and Will were to consider marriage, they would have to discuss many things.

And then there was the most difficult part of all. What about *Mamm*? Who would take care of her, now that *Dat* was gone? As the oldest of the *kinner*, she felt a responsibility to care for *Mamm*. After all, *Mamm* and *Dat* had always cared for her. Could she just leave behind everything to live for her own selfish desires? She didn't think so.

Perhaps she should break things off with Will and consider John Glick's proposal. John was certainly more suited to her. He was Amish. He knew how to farm and enjoyed it, unlike William, who had no clue about farming.

But wasn't there more to a marriage than just farming and being Amish? She didn't care for John the way she cared for Will – the way she loved Will. *Yes*, she realized, *I love William,* and that fact alone was more pertinent than all of the others combined.

Could I just walk away from Will now that I've discovered our love? Certainly not. It was then she realized there was no power on earth stronger than the power they shared between them: the power of love.

William couldn't get his uncle's words out of his head. What did he mean by 'unequally yoked'? He searched through the concordance next to his Bible until he came to the passage that mentioned the phrase. There was only one.

He quickly opened his Bible and flipped to the verse in Second Corinthians and silently read the words. *Be ye not un-equally yoked together with unbelievers: for what fellowship hath righteousness with unrighteousness? And what commu-nion hath light with darkness?*

What was Uncle George implying by recommending these verses to him? Did his uncle think that Sally wasn't saved? *Is she saved?* Didn't the Amish basically believe the same things that Christians do?

This only meant one thing: he'd have to study more and talk to Sally about her beliefs.

William sighed. He loved Sally like no other person on earth, but his love for God trumped all else.

FIVE

"Saloma, *kumm*." As soon as the younger *maed* had gone to bed, *Mamm* beckoned to Saloma. The urgency in *Mamm's* voice frightened Saloma.

What could be wrong? Had *Mamm* discovered that she'd been seeing William? Had someone in their community seen them together?

Mamm waved her near, a look of disappointment in her eyes. "*Ach*, Saloma."

The tears in her mother's eyes brought tears rushing to the surface of Saloma's eyes too.

What would she say? "*Mamm*, I–"

"Don't say anything. Just read this." She quickly drew an envelope from her apron pocket.

Saloma unfolded what appeared to be an official document of some kind. Her eyes skimmed the words on the page, but they were so technical she scarcely understood their meaning. "What does this mean?"

"They want to take our land away."

Saloma gasped. "What? How can they do that?"

"This paper says this land belongs to someone else."

"That's a lie! *Dat's vatter* bought this land."

A helpless look crossed *Mamm's* face. "It says that your *vatter* gave this land away."

None of this made any sense. "*Dat* would not give our land away!"

"Saloma, it is true. A lawyer came by the house today and delivered these papers. He explained it all to me."

"Explained what? I don't understand any of this, *Mamm.*"

Mamm took a deep breath and looked Saloma in the eye. "This is going to be difficult to hear, *dochder.* I've been trying to figure it out since the man came. It didn't make any sense. I don't know why your father never told me." A tear slipped down *Mamm's* cheek. She grasped Saloma's hand for strength.

"*Mamm?*"

"Seems your *vatter* had another *fraa* before me. It was before we ever met."

Utter shock coursed through Saloma's being. Her father had been married before? She shook her head. "I don't believe it, *Mamm.* That man is a liar! It's not true!"

Her mother took her hands in her own. "It is. He has papers to prove it."

"What do papers mean? They mean nothing to me."

"In the eyes of the law, they are everything. We could fight it, but he said it would just cost us a lot of money. And we would probably lose anyway."

"Did you talk to the bishop? What did he say?"

"No. I will speak with him about this tomorrow."

Saloma bit her fingernail, debating whether to speak what was on her mind. "*Mamm*, I...I know someone. He...uh...is *Englisch*. Maybe he can help us. His uncle is someone important, I think."

"Saloma, what are you saying? Who are you talking about?"

"I have an *Englisch* friend. I will talk to him about this."

"No. I don't want you talking about our business with some strange *Englischer*. I will talk with the bishop. He will know what to do."

Saloma nodded, then spoke the words that had been on her mind. "*Mamm*, what if they do take our home away? What will we do?"

Tears filled *Mamm's* eyes once again. "I don't know, *dochder*. I just don't know why your *vatter* would have done this." *Mamm's* voice broke off in a sob, and Saloma drew her close.

Dear Gott, *what are we going to do?*

Saloma's heart raced as she dialed the number Will had given her. He'd said that, if she ever needed to call him for anything, she shouldn't hesitate to do so. She closed the door to the phone shanty to be certain no one would hear her conversation.

"Hello?"

Relief washed over her when Will answered on the second ring. Just the sound of his voice soothed her frayed nerves.

"Sally? Is that you?" Concern echoed through his words.

"*Jah*, Will," Saloma choked back tears.

"Is something wrong?"

"*Jah*. Very wrong."

Panic seized his voice. "What is it? Are you hurt?"

"*Nee*. It's not like that," Saloma reassured him. "I-I need to talk to you." She sniffled.

"Wait right there. I'll come get you."

She quickly thought of a place where he could pick her up. "Do you know where our vegetable stand is? Can you meet me there?"

"Yes, I'm coming right now."

"*Denki*." She put the phone back into the receiver with a shaky hand. Hopefully no one would see Will picking her up out at the stand. She figured that was the most secluded place on the property.

Property that would soon belong to a stranger.

William yanked his button-down flannel from its hanger and hastily slipped his arms in. The evenings were sometimes chilly, and this night was no exception. He grabbed the Jeep keys from his dresser and slid them into his pants pocket then quickly made his way down the hall. He attempted to keep his anxious thoughts at bay.

"Going somewhere?" Uncle George's voice echoed from the great room.

This was not the time for a discussion. "Yes. I'm going out for a while."

"It's a little late, don't you think?"

"I realize that." William grimaced. How many questions was Uncle George going to ask?

"How long will you be?"

William glanced at his watch. It was nearly ten-thirty. "I don't know."

"Where are you going?"

He felt like telling Uncle George it was none of his business, but attempted not to show disrespect. "Listen, I don't have a lot of time to talk. I'll have my cell phone if you need to get a hold of me. I need to go now." He thought about Sally waiting outside for him.

"Meeting a woman at this time of night is not a good idea, William."

If he wanted to argue, they could do that later. Right now, the most important thing was getting to Sally.

"Bye, Uncle George." William quickly slipped out the door.

What could be wrong with Sally? Why did she sound so distraught over the phone? Imagining every possible calamity, his wandering mind caused him to accelerate a little faster.

As Will turned the corner, he noticed a buggy was stopped in front of Sally's roadside stand. Should he approach, or should he wait until the buggy left? Sally glanced his way. If only he knew what she was thinking.

Maybe he would just drive by. No, that might not be the best idea. What if his presence would cause trouble for her?

Will pulled off the road and waited. He watched intently as Sally politely listened to the person in the buggy. Hopefully, it wasn't her bishop.

He noticed an arm reach out from the buggy and grasp Sally's hand. The hair rose on his neck. Was there a young man in the buggy? Sally glanced his way again then back to the person in the buggy. William began to feel uneasy. Was someone trying to hit on Sally?

A moment later, Sally stepped back from the buggy and the wheels began to turn. Will watched as the buggy disappeared over a hill. He turned the engine over and approached the roadside stand.

"Sally?" His eyes met hers, and he felt the spark that had been so evident since the day they'd met. Sally briefly smiled then jogged around to the passenger's side and hopped into his Jeep. William reached over and grasped her hand. "You okay?"

She offered a slight nod that told William something was indeed wrong, but she was dealing with it.

He thought about the man in the buggy and decided it'd be best to bring that up at a later time. Still, another man holding Sally's hand just didn't sit right with him.

He glanced at Sally. "Want to talk about it?"

She nodded and took a cleansing breath, it seemed. "It's about our home. *Ach*, it's kind of a long story."

Will reached to the dashboard and turned up the heater. "Are you cold?"

"A little, *jah*."

"I wish I could take you back to my place but my uncle..." He wasn't about to tell her that his uncle had a disdain for Amish people. "It's just better if we're not there when he's home. We can park somewhere."

"That's *gut*."

William pulled into the library's parking lot and parked near a street lamp. He turned to Sally. "Tell me what's wrong. I've got all night, if you need me." He meant it, too. Right now, nothing in this world mattered more than this special woman at his side.

Sally managed a slight smile and lightly stroked his face. "*Denki*." She took another breath. "My *vatter*..." That was when the tears came.

William would have pulled her into his arms, but to do so in his vehicle would be awkward. Instead, he reached over and held her hand. He waited in silence for her to continue.

"He...he was married. Before my *mamm*. She never knew about it."

William frowned. "Your father had been married before?"

"It was a long time ago. We think he probably got a divorce, but we're unsure. Anyway, he made some papers, you know, that said that if he died, his possessions would belong to her."

"A will?"

"*Jah*, that's what *Mamm* said it was called."

"But the will didn't include *your* family?" The thought was preposterous. Why would a man leave everything he owned to someone other than his family?

"Only his first family."

"I don't understand. Why would he do that?"

"We don't know. Maybe he forgot that he signed those papers."

Will shook his head. "I can't believe it. Was he institutionalized or something?"

"I don't know what that means."

"Did he spend time in a hospital? Maybe he was in the military and was wounded."

Sally shrugged. "Amish don't believe in joining the military."

"They don't?" This was a shock. Somehow he'd missed that bit of knowledge while researching.

"*Nee*. It is not right to kill another person; the Bible says so."

He wasn't about to argue with Sally. There were more important matters at stake right now. He filed the subject in the back of his mind to bring up in a later discussion.

"It sounds like you need to hire a lawyer," Will suggested.

"*Nee*, I don't think we can do that. The bishop and ministers won't allow it."

"You're kidding. They'll just let whoever take your land away from you? That's not right."

"I know. I want to do something, but I don't know what or how."

William thought about Uncle George. There was no way he'd take this case. "I can talk to my uncle, but I don't think he would represent you. Maybe he can give us some advice, though."

"Your uncle?"

"He's a lawyer."

"Is that why he lives in such a fancy house?"

William nodded. "He makes a lot of money."

Sally frowned. "We don't have a lot of money to pay him. My *vatter* left us some, and I will probably get a job soon to make more. *Mamm* and I have talked about it."

"No. I wouldn't want you to use your money for a lawyer." He reached over and caressed her cheek.

"I don't know what we'll do if they take our house."

"Do you have relatives you could stay with?"

"In Kentucky."

William's heart sank. *Kentucky?* "I couldn't stand it if you moved away."

"If we had to, it would be because *Der Herr* wills it."

"And what if *Der Herr* wills that I marry you first?"

Sally grew quiet. Why did she do that whenever he brought up a future together?

He lifted her chin, encouraging eye-contact. "Sally, why are you silent? Would you not consider marrying me in the future?"

"We're just so different."

"Isn't that a good thing? It would be boring if we were exactly alike."

"You do not understand our ways. I am not allowed to marry an *Englischer.*"

"Do you love me, Sally?"

"*Jah*, but—"

William's fingers on her lips stopped her words. "No buts, Sally. I love you and you love me. If we have love, we can work *anything* out."

"I think it is more difficult than you think it is."

"I didn't say it wouldn't be difficult. I know it won't be easy. But it *is* possible."

"Do you think my *vatter* loved his first *fraa*?"

"I don't know, but I'm guessing he did or he wouldn't have drawn up a will."

"If it didn't work out for them, what makes us think it will work out for us?"

Will reached over and grasped Sally's hand. "I don't know what happened with them, but I can say for a fact that I will never *ever* leave the woman I marry. I can promise you that."

"You don't know the future."

"I don't have to. I know that I love you."

"*Ach*, Will."

He leaned over and brushed his lips against hers.

SIX

William waited until most of the congregation had cleared the auditorium before he approached Pastor Rob. He was in need of spiritual guidance, and he wasn't about to get it from Uncle George. His father had once alluded that Uncle George used to work in the ministry with him, but William had never seen any evidence of that. On the contrary, he seemed about as far away from God as anyone out in the world.

"William, good to see you this morning." The pastor shook his hand.

"That was a compelling sermon."

"Yep. I think I needed to hear it more than anyone."

"My father used to say that often." William smiled.

"He was a wise man and a great preacher. I learned a lot from him."

"Yeah, me too."

"Did you want to talk about something?"

Will nodded.

"Let's go have a seat." Pastor Rob led the way to a secluded cluster of chairs near the back of the auditorium. "What's on your mind?"

"I've been seeing a girl. She's Amish."

The pastor's forehead wrinkled and he nodded for William to continue.

"I guess what I wanted to ask is, would I be unequally yoked if I married her?"

"That depends. Is she saved?"

"Well, the research I conducted on Amish beliefs stated that they believe in Jesus."

Pastor Rob frowned. "Research? Salvation is an individual thing. It's a matter of the heart."

"I realize that."

"Have you asked her if she's received Christ as *her* Saviour?"

"No, sir."

"Then I'd say that's where you need to start."

"Okay." William nodded. "I have another question. Do we have any positions available? You know, I've been taking classes in counseling."

"I'm afraid the only position we need to fill here is that of custodian."

"Custodian? You mean someone to clean the church, right?"

The pastor nodded. "It doesn't pay much."

"What are the hours?"

"It would just be two days a week; Mondays and Thursdays."

"Could I get the job?" William scratched his head. "I would probably bring my girlfriend to help. The job would actually be for her, but I'd help out. She needs the money."

"I hear the Amish are pretty good housekeepers. I'll talk to our staff and get back with you tomorrow."

"Great. Thanks, Pastor." William firmly shook Pastor Rob's hand.

"No problem."

William smiled. Wouldn't Sally be happy!

He'd been pondering the situation for some time now, but William was still reticent to speak with Uncle George regarding Sally's family. What if he put the question in theoretical terms? Would his uncle know that he was speaking of an Amish family's plight? Either way, he had to try to get answers for Sally.

At present, Uncle George was working in his office. William never bothered him while he was working; it was a rule they'd agreed upon when his uncle took him in. Hopefully, he'd finish up his work before William turned in for the night.

William yawned and retrieved his Bible from his nightstand. Pastor Rob's message about staying in God's Word penetrated his heart. He'd gotten away from his daily reading, and felt lately that he'd been dragging, spiritually-speaking. Time with God in His Word was the only cure.

About thirty minutes later, Uncle George began rustling papers, and William took that as his cue. As his uncle neared his door, William stepped out into the hallway.

"I've been wanting to talk to you about something," William said.

"Sure. Let's take a seat in the den."

"First of all, I'd like to apologize for my attitude lately."

His uncle's brow arched and he nodded.

"I read the passage in the Bible that you suggested, and I plan to talk to Sally about it soon."

"Sally?"

"My girlfriend."

Uncle George frowned.

He'd better get to the point quickly before his uncle started another argument. "I want to ask you something. I have a friend who is getting their house taken away because of a will. Apparently, my friend's dad had been married before he met my friend's mom, and he had a will. The will didn't include his current family, only the family that he had many years ago."

His uncle nodded.

"Is there any way that they'd be able to fight it? I mean, would it do any good?"

"That depends on a lot of factors. I'd have to see the terminology used in the will."

"I was thinking that, since my friend's family has lived on the property for many years, doesn't that give them the rights to it? What is that saying? Possession is nine-tenths of the law."

"Like I said, that would depend on several factors."

"How would I figure that out?"

"You'd have to get a copy of the will, look for loopholes, that sort of thing."

"Would you be willing to help me?"

Uncle George rubbed his forehead. "Who did you say this was for?"

"I didn't. It's for a friend."

"I'm sorry, William. I don't think I can help you."

"Why not?"

"First of all, you're being very vague. I'm guessing this has something to do with the Amish girl. Am I correct?"

William shook his head. "Forget I even asked." He stood up and began walking to his room. "Goodnight, Uncle George."

A light knock sounded on Will's door a few moments later.

William looked at the door and sighed. "Come in."

Uncle George stood in the door's opening. "Despite what you may think, William, I'm not trying to ruin your life." He rubbed his cheek. "I'm not your enemy."

"I know."

"Your father and I were good friends. Before he ever met your mother."

Will nodded.

"I introduced them. William, there's a lot that you don't know about your parents…things they may not have wanted you to know."

"Like what?"

"Well, I'm not sure this is the right time to tell you." His uncle shook his head. "I probably shouldn't say anything."

"Why on earth did you bring it up, then?" William didn't mask his frustrated tone.

"I guess what I'm trying to say is that you need to trust me. Nobody knew your parents like I did."

"Why did you turn your back on God?"

Uncle George frowned. "I haven't turned my back on God. I'm just sorting through some things right now."

"Uncle George, would you like to attend church with me on Sunday?"

"No thank you, William."

SEVEN

*S*aloma heard it from the kitchen. She rushed toward *Mamm's* room to find her mother kneeling beside her bed. Loud sobbing escaped *Mamm's* lips, and her body heaved in sorrow. Saloma knelt next to her mother and wrapped her arms around her.

"*Mamm*?"

"Why? Why would he do this?"

"I don't know." A tear trailed down Saloma's cheek. She could only imagine the pain her mother felt.

"I had no idea, Saloma. No idea at all."

"About *Dat* being married before?"

"About any of it. The will. His former marriage. You think he would have told me *something*. Why would he hide these secrets?"

"Maybe he thought you wouldn't marry him if you knew."

"I never kept any secrets from your *vatter*. Never." She brushed away a tear. "How could he do this to me? To us?"

"I don't know. Do you think maybe he forgot that he signed a will? I cannot see *Dat* leaving us with nothing. He wouldn't have done that."

"I don't know. I'm beginning to think I did not know your father at all."

"That's not true, *Mamm*. You did know *Dat*."

"We'd been married for twenty-two years, Saloma. You'd think that it would have come up in conversation. I'm certain he hadn't forgotten about a wife! And, what if..." Her mother frowned. "What if they had children?"

"You don't think *Dat* would abandon his own *kinner*."

"I don't know what to think anymore, Saloma."

"*Mamm*, *Dat* loved you. He loved all of us," Saloma reassured. "You have to believe that."

William carried a tray with two tall glasses of iced tea. He set it down on the small side table beside the couch in his uncle's library.

"Mm, those look refreshing." Sally's appreciative smile concreted one of the reasons he adored her.

"I was unsure if you wanted sugar, so I had Marita put some in a dish for us." He handed a glass to Sally and took a sip of his own. He made a face. "Yikes, this does need sugar."

"You shouldn't need any sugar; you're already sweet enough."

"You need to get to know me better," he teased.

"*Ach*, I already know it's true." Sally spooned two heaps into her own drink. "This is *gut*."

He rounded the sofa and sat down next to Sally. Will remembered his phone conversation yesterday. "Hey, guess what? I have news for you."

"Did you talk to your uncle about my house?" Sally's face brightened.

"Yes, but that's not what this is about. Guess again."

"Uh…" She shrugged.

"I got us a job!"

"Us?"

He nodded. "I asked my pastor if they had any openings, and he said that they needed someone to clean the church twice a week."

"Only twice a week?"

"I know it's not much, but it's something, right? And we can pretty much work on our own schedule, so whenever it's convenient."

"You – you did this for me?" Sally's eyes widened.

"Yeah. I mean, I guess there might be some selfish motives in there; I'll get to see you more often. What do you think?"

"I think it's wonderful. But I'll have to talk to my *mamm* about it."

"Okay."

"She doesn't know about you." She bit her fingernail. "I don't know what she would do if she knew we were courting."

He quirked a brow. "Courting?"

Sally nodded.

He lifted his hand to caress her earlobe. "You're so cute."

Beautiful color blushed her cheeks.

"Come here," he beckoned, pulling her close.

Sally did as requested.

His lips moved just inches from hers, and he detected long-ing in her eyes. "You know, I've never seen your hair down. Will you show me?"

She nodded reservedly then began removing the pins that held her prayer *kapp* in place. As she removed the pins that held her bun in place, her locks tumbled down around her shoulders and back. Her hesitant mien begged for affirmation.

"Oh, Sally." His gaze smoldered. "You're even more beauti-ful than I imagined. And I have a pretty good imagination."

"I – I've never uncovered my head for someone."

Did she mean that he was the first man who had the privi-lege of seeing her with her hair down? What a wonderful gift she'd given him. He lightly stroked her soft tresses and drew her mouth to his. Her lips tasted of the sweet tea they'd enjoyed just moments ago.

Sally pulled back momentarily for a breath then resumed contact once again. Will pulled her even closer until there was no distance left between them. His hands wove through her hair and down her back. Will leaned forward onto the sofa with Sal-ly beside him. He soon realized that he might not be able to stop if they went any further. But stopping was so difficult when it seemed neither of them had the desire to.

"William!" Uncle George's voice shouted from the library's entrance.

Will and Sally both shot up.

Oh, no.

"Get that tramp out of my house!" His uncle's blazing glare pierced Sally's guilt-ridden eyes. "Now!"

Sally looked at Will helplessly, and tears immediately pooled in their depths.

William chided himself. *How could I be so stupid!*

"Uncle George–"

"Get her out," he thrust his finger toward the door, "and don't ever bring her back again!"

Will's apologetic gaze met Sally's and he mouthed the words *I'm sorry.* He grabbed her hand and they both fled past Uncle George. The sooner they left the house, the better. Hopefully, Uncle George will have calmed down by the time he returned.

Sally's hands shook nervously as they jogged to Will's Jeep. "Oh, no; I forgot my hair pins and *kapp*! I can't go home without them."

Will grasped her hand reassuringly. "I'll get it." He turned to look at her. "It'll be all right, Sally. Don't worry."

"Are – are you sure?"

"I'm not afraid of my uncle."

"He doesn't sound like a kind man."

"He has his moments. Don't worry about it. I'll deal with him." He lightly caressed her shoulder. "Will you be okay out here?"

Sally nodded.

Will turned from the vehicle and headed back toward the house. He hesitated and turned back toward her. "It'll be okay, Sally."

Did he say that to reassure her or himself?

William took a cleansing breath and whispered a brief prayer before re-entering his uncle's home. He hurried toward the library, hoping to avoid another confrontation with his uncle. However, fate would have it another way, it seemed.

"What on earth are you doing, William?" Uncle George's scowl was evident in his tone.

"I'm getting Sally's *kapp*," Will kept his voice even and calmly walked to the sofa.

His uncle sneered, "That's not what I was referring to and you know it."

William clenched his fist and turned to his uncle. "You may not approve of Sally, but you have no right to call her derogatory names!"

"I'll say and do *whatever* I please in my own home. And if you intend on bringing that *trash* onto my property again–"

Uncle George's words halted when his mouth was met with William's fist. Blood trickled from his lip, onto his freshly-pressed shirt.

"Get out now, before I do something we'll both regret!" his uncle demanded.

William said nothing, turned an about face, and walked out the door.

EIGHT

William reached over and grasped Saloma's hand. "Thank you for coming with me to church today. Pastor Rob can't wait to meet you."

"I'm kind of nervous." Sally glanced down at her Amish attire.

"Don't be. I'll be right next to you the entire time."

"The whole time? But you will not sit with me on the ladies' side." She laughed.

"The ladies' side? What do you mean?"

"You will sit with the men, and I will sit with the women."

Will's eyes widened, and he finally realized her meaning. "Do men and women sit in different places in Amish church?"

"*Jah.* It is not like this in your church?"

William chuckled. "Nope. We sit wherever we want to, and I intend to sit as close to you as possible."

Sally gasped. "While the bishop is speaking?"

"We just have a pastor, and, yes, I plan to hold your hand during the service."

"Do the men go in first?"

"Go in?"

"Into the building where meeting is."

"We're going to walk into the church just like we'd walk into the library or a store or a restaurant. Together. The men and women are not separated unless they want to be."

"Oh."

Will chuckled. "I guess this will be a new experience for you."

"*Jah.* For sure and certain."

Will leaned over and whispered, "What do you think?"

Sally smiled. "He has good words. I like what he is saying."

That's good. Sally was listening to the sermon. William turned his attention back to Pastor Rob's message and nonchalantly draped his arm around Sally's shoulders.

She gasped and leaned over. "This is okay?"

Will smiled and nodded. He noticed Sally looking around at others in the auditorium, probably trying to determine whether they were as shocked as she was at William's innocent public display of affection. She quickly refocused her attention on the pulpit.

Ten minutes later, they stood and sang a closing hymn. Will introduced Sally to a few members and shook hands with several people.

Will glanced at Sally. "Are you ready to go?"

"Go? It is over already?" Sally's mouth dropped open. "It has only been one hour."

"Yep." William smiled. "Let's go get some lunch."

Sally's eyes seemed to be searching for something. "Do they eat in here?"

"No, sweetheart. We don't have lunch at the church unless it's a special occasion. I meant I'm going to take you out to a restaurant."

"Oh."

"Did you hear Pastor Rob? He said we could start our job this week." They walked to his Jeep hand-in-hand, and Will opened her door.

"*Jah*. That is *gut*."

"Did you talk to your mom yet?"

Sally frowned. "I don't know what to say to her. I mean, I told her about the job and that I have a ride with an *Englisch* friend. But she doesn't know that you're my beau."

"Your beau, huh?" Will's eyes sparkled at her endearing term. "Well, we *are* friends too."

"*Jah*. That's true." She gently pulled on her *kapp* string. "I'm afraid, if I tell her, she will forbid me to see you."

"Sounds like my uncle."

"Has he forbidden you to see me?"

"No. I'm a grown man. He doesn't have that authority over me." He caressed her cheek. "And, if he did, I'm certain I would defy it."

"You would defy your uncle's authority?" Will detected surprise in Sally's voice.

"If it was the only way I could be with you, then, yes. But it doesn't matter, because he doesn't have that authority." Will rubbed his chin. "I don't know why, but for some reason he is against the Amish."

"All Amish, or against me?"

"No, it's not you. I'm certain that if you weren't Amish, he'd love you."

"Do you want me to become *Englisch*?" Sally became quiet.

"We haven't discussed that yet, have we?" He briefly glanced at her. "It's something I've been wanting to talk to you about. I guess I've just been afraid to bring it up. I don't want to lose you."

"I don't know if I can become an *Englischer*."

"It's not the Amish – *Englisch* thing that bothers me. My main concern is our faith. We *have to* agree on what we believe, because, if we ever marry and have children, they will need to be taught, and we have to be in agreement." Will stroked her hand. "Sally, what *do* you believe?"

Sally kept quiet for a moment. "About God?"

William nodded.

"Well, I believe in God and His Son Jesus."

"And what about Heaven? How do you get to Heaven?"

"By believing in Jesus and doing my best and following the *Ordnung*."

Will's brow lowered. "What is the *Ordnung*?"

"It's our rules. You know, about dressing proper and all that."

"So, they're ordinances." He nodded. "And if you believe in God and Jesus and keep these rules, then you can go to Heaven?" His brow shot up.

"Well, I don't know. Only God can say for certain sure. I won't know until I stand before Him."

"God *did* say, in His Word. He said that when we trust in what Christ did on the cross, that those ordinances do not affect us. They were nailed to the cross with Jesus. Ordinances, or laws, cannot get you to Heaven unless you obey them perfectly. And I don't know anyone who's perfect except Jesus."

"That's why we have to believe in Jesus too, ain't so?"

"Well, the Bible says that the law can't make you right with God. The Apostle Paul said, *I do not frustrate the grace of God: for if righteousness come by the law, then Christ is dead in vain.* And he says that, *A man is not justified by the works of the law, but by the faith of Jesus Christ, even we have believed in Jesus Christ, that we might be justified by the faith of Christ, and not by the works of the law: for by the works of the law shall no flesh be justified.*"

"So, are you saying that I don't need to be a good person and keep the laws?"

"That is not necessary to go to Heaven. All you need is to place your faith in Jesus Christ." Will smiled. "Good people don't go to Heaven; saved people do."

"But, if I put my faith in Jesus, I still have to do what's right. I can't just go and steal something or kill someone. Those things would be wrong."

"I agree that those things are wrong, and we shouldn't do them. God doesn't want us to sin, ever. But, as human beings, we will sin. The Bible puts it this way, *Shall we continue in sin that grace may abound? God forbid.* Sin is always sinful and wrong." Will rubbed his forehead. "But once we place our trust in Jesus, we become children of God. We are born again – a new creature. We belong to God. God will never leave us nor forsake us, no matter what we do."

"But what about our sin? I thought we couldn't go to Heaven if we sin."

"That is true, but, as a child of God and a believer in Christ, *all* of your sins have been paid for. Jesus Christ took the penalty for all your sins – past, present, and future. So, when you stand before God, it's like Jesus is standing in your place.

"If you ask God, 'What about my sin?' He will look at you and say, 'What sin? There is none here.' He has removed your sins as far as the east is from the west, and He remembers them no more. This is all in the Bible. I can show you if you'd like."

"I would like that. Not that I don't believe you; I do. I would just like to see it for myself."

"I totally understand. I wouldn't want you to take my word for it. When the disciples preached to the Bereans, they searched the Scriptures to see if what the disciples were saying was true.

I think we should be like the Bereans and always do that, because there's nothing more important than the Truth."

Sally seemed to ponder his words.

"And, by the way, the Bible also says that you can *know* that you have eternal life. You don't have to wait until you stand before God."

Sally gasped. "Where does it say that? I've never heard that before."

"It's in 1 John 5:17. It says, *These things have I written unto you that believe on the name of the Son of God; that ye may know that ye have eternal life.* We can look it up later. But I think God wrote that down because He wants us to have confidence in Him. We cannot truly have peace in our hearts if we're always wondering if we're really saved or not. I'm glad that God wrote it down in black and white."

"Will, I want to become a child of God."

"You do?" Joy filled his heart.

"*Jah.* How do I do it?"

"It's very simple. *If thou shalt confess with thy mouth the Lord Jesus, and shalt believe in thine heart that God hath raised him from the dead, thou shalt be saved.*"

"I will do that right now." Sally smiled and quietly bowed her head. "I confess the Lord Jesus with my mouth and I believe that God raised Him from the dead too. Please save me. Amen." Sally looked up at William, tears in her eyes. "I did it!"

"Yes, you did. Praise the Lord!" He reached up and caressed her cheek. "I don't think I can ever love anyone more than you."

"How about God?"

"Well, I wasn't counting Him. He is everything." He playfully pulled her *kapp* string. "You are second."

"I don't mind being second."

Will pulled Sally close and claimed her lips. "Good."

NINE

William wracked his brain, desperate to find a way to help Sally's family keep their property. Sally had given him a copy of the alleged will, but he couldn't make heads or tails of all the legal jargon. He wondered if maybe someone was trying to pull a scam on the Troyer family. He'd taken the will to Uncle George, but his uncle was unwilling to help Sally's family, to Will's chagrin.

What would Sally and her family do if they lost their home? William couldn't bear the thought of Sally moving away. If he was finished with school, it wouldn't be such a big deal. He would move anywhere to be with Sally. But this semester wouldn't end for a few months, and he couldn't go anywhere until he earned his degree he'd been working so hard for over the last few years.

Sally seemed to enjoy working at the church, and he enjoyed the extra time with her, although janitorial duties were not his profession of choice. Since Sally received Christ, William noticed a change in her, though subtle. She seemed happier. Even so, William also detected concern in her demeanor. She carried around an invisible weight. William determined to speak with her about this the next time they worked together, which would be today.

He pulled into Sally's long driveway and waited for her to emerge from the house. He found it somewhat surprising that her mother allowed her to travel with an *Englisch* man, although she wasn't privy to their romantic relationship, as far as he knew. If Sally's mother did know, he was quite certain she'd put a stop to their relationship altogether.

"Hey, beautiful!" He smiled as Sally slid into the passenger's seat and closed the door. He longed to lean close and plant a kiss on her lips, but wouldn't dare until they were in a more private setting.

Sally's cheeks darkened. It seemed she wasn't use to a lot of attention, which Will loved to lavish on her.

"Any news on the house?"

"*Mamm* spoke with Bishop Mast. He's going to talk to a lawyer about it and see what can be done."

He reached over and stroked her hand. "I'm sorry my uncle won't help."

"It's not your fault, Will. You have tried, ain't so?"

"Yeah. I just don't know what I can do. If I had the knowledge or the resources my uncle has, I'm sure I could help with something. And, if you did lose the house, I would invite you to stay with us, but my uncle would never allow anything of the sort."

"Well, that would be a *gut* thing. I don't know if you and I could live in the same house."

"You're right. We'd have to get married." He smiled.

"I don't know how this is going to work."

Will frowned. "With the house or us?"

"Either."

"I'm curious about something, Sally. What did your bishop say about you having received Christ?"

"*Ach*, I could never tell him!"

Will's chin dropped. "Why ever not? Don't you think he'd want to know?"

Sally looked mortified. "Bishop Mast? *Nee*. He shunned his own *dochder,* Sarah, over that very thing."

"I don't understand. I would think a bishop would be thrilled to hear something like that." He scratched his head. "So, you have to keep silent about your faith?"

Sally nodded.

"But Christ commands us, as Christians, to share our faith. I don't know if I could just sit by and watch my family die, knowing that they could be on their way to Hell. Even if I couldn't speak the words to them, I'd at least write them a letter or give them a Gospel tract – something – to warn them."

"But I'm not allowed to speak of these things."

"We ought to obey God, rather than men. If you have to choose between following Jesus and obeying the Amish church, I sincerely hope you'll choose Jesus. Sally, the Amish church didn't hang on the cross for you. Jesus said, *I am the way, the truth, and the life. No man cometh unto the Father but by me.* Don't you think your family and the other members of your church have a right to know how to get to Heaven?"

"I don't think they would believe it."

"It is not our job to make them believe. That part is between them and God. Our part is to tell them. We do not have control or responsibility over how others respond." He rubbed her shoulder. "And who knows? *You* received Christ. Who's to say *they* won't?"

"I'm afraid to. I wouldn't know what to say to them."

"How did you get saved, Sally?"

"I just confessed with my mouth and believed in my heart that Jesus died for me on the cross and arose from the dead on the third day."

"Why did you do that?"

"Because I want to go to Heaven."

"That's all you need to know, sweetheart. Those are the words of life. There's nothing magical, no special combination of words you need to say. The thief on the cross next to Jesus only said *Lord, remember me when thou comest into thy kingdom.* His words weren't anything special, but Jesus saw the sincerity of his heart."

Sally nodded. "It will be difficult for me."

"I know. That's okay, though. God will be with you every step of the way, holding your hand."

Saloma quietly stirred the pot of chicken vegetable soup, pondering the day spent with William. Will was everything she'd ever dreamed about in a mate – kind, caring, handsome. He treated her like a princess. Marrying him would be like living in a fairy tale, for sure and certain.

She glanced toward the living area when she heard a knock on the door, but couldn't see who had come to call. She strained to hear the voice. The person her mother spoke with was clearly male.

"Sally." It was the only thing she heard. She set the wooden spoon on the warming rack and hurried toward the door.

"There is no Sally here," she heard her mother respond.

"*Mamm*," she looked to her mother, then to William's uncle, "I think he's here to speak to me."

Will's uncle nodded. "That's right."

"We can step outside," Saloma suggested, hoping her mother wouldn't ask any questions. "*Mamm*, I left the soup on the stove. Someone should probably stir it."

Saloma watched her mother nod hesitantly, her gaze curious. She quickly stepped outside with William's uncle and closed the door behind them.

She leveled her gaze at the man. "Why did you come here?"

He frowned. "Am I not welcome?"

"You have been unkind to me, so I'm guessing this isn't a social visit." She crossed her arms over her chest.

"I've underestimated your intelligence. You're right, it's not a social visit." He raised an eyebrow. "I have a proposition for you."

TEN

William thumbed through the pages of his psychology textbook, searching for the answer to a question in his coursework. It seemed as though school had become more difficult since he'd met Sally. He had trouble concentrating on his studies, as his mind often became preoccupied with thoughts of her. However, if he had any hope of marrying her, he must complete his schooling and earn his degree so he could get a decent-paying job, should God bless them with a family in the future.

A soft knock on his door prompted an answer.

"Come in," he bade.

Marita opened the door several inches and stood in the doorway. "Mr. Griffith, your uncle requested your presence at the dinner table."

"Please tell him I'm not hungry, Marita." The statement wasn't entirely true. He could stand to eat a meal, but he'd been avoiding his uncle's presence as much as possible lately.

He'd grab a bite alone later, when Uncle George retired for the evening.

"He asked me not to return without you, sir."

William sighed. Why did Uncle George have to involve Marita in their tussles? It wasn't fair to her, and William knew his uncle often used Marita as leverage to get him to do his bidding.

"Okay, Marita." William stuck the class notes he'd taken into his textbook and closed it, and then hopped off his chaise. He followed Marita down the hallway and into the dining room.

Uncle George folded the newspaper he'd been reading and set it beside his plate. He removed his reading glasses and pinched the bridge of his nose.

Will's eyes narrowed. "You wanted to see me?"

"Yes, William. We don't see each other all that often. I'd like you to at least have supper with me when you *are* home."

William frowned. "I was studying." *Attempting* to study would have been more accurate.

"You need to eat too. Take a seat."

Will nodded and obediently sat at the table, opposite Uncle George. Three chairs separated them on each side of the table, and William had always wondered why his uncle owned such a large table for just the two of them.

"How are your classes coming along?"

"Fine."

"It's a wonder you have time to study anymore these days."

"What's that supposed to mean?" Will's jaw clenched.

"It seems to me that your attention has shifted to other, less important, things lately."

"First of all, Sally is not a *thing*. Second, you're crazy if you think school is more important than she is. Third, like I've told you before, my relationship with Sally is none of your business."

"Indeed. William, I'm trying to protect you from the mistake of a lifetime."

"Please don't. I'm entitled to make my own mistakes, aren't I? I plan to marry Sally one day. There's nothing you can say to change my mind."

"William," Uncle George sighed, "the Amish, their family ties are strong. She'll leave you and go back to them."

"No, she won't. She loves me."

"William, trust me on this one. It's happened time and time again. Love is not a factor."

How could his uncle say love was not a factor? Of course, it was! The biggest factor of all. Had his uncle once loved an Amish woman? Did he get his heart broken? Is that why he was so adamant against their union?

"It won't happen to us." He was confident of it.

"I know you don't *think* it will, William. But what if it does? What *if* she leaves you?"

William thought for a few seconds. "If she leaves, I'll have to follow her."

"And give up everything you've worked so hard for?" Uncle George rubbed his forehead. "Your parents set aside a lot of money for you to go to school."

"Is anything more important than love?"

William smiled as he glanced at the small stuffed bear in the passenger's seat. He couldn't wait to see Sally light up when he gave it to her in just a few moments. However, the bear wasn't the most special part about his gift; it was the promise ring that sat in the box the bear held in its paws. Although it would probably be a while before they actually married, Will wanted to give her something to let her know that she belonged to him exclusively. He knew she wouldn't be able to wear the ring while she was still Amish, as that was against their rules, but he wanted her to have it just the same.

When he turned down the road that led to Sally's driveway, he immediately noticed two of her sisters in the garden. Hopefully they hadn't found out about his and Sally's intimate relationship. Sally could explain that to everyone when she was good and ready. For now, they would just take their relationship in stride as far as her family was concerned.

He saw one of Sally's sisters run into the house at the sight of his Jeep. Was she going to get Sally or alert her to his presence? One of Sally's sisters met Will at the Jeep.

"Is Sally here?" He smiled at the timid girls.

One of them shook her head silently. The other one handed him an envelope. Both girls turned and hurried back to the house.

William frowned and looked toward the house. Did this mean Sally wasn't able to come to work today? Why hadn't she called him from the phone shanty?

He studied the envelope in his hands. Perhaps his answer lied within. He opened the envelope and pulled out a single sheet of paper. His eyes scanned the words at first, then he realized the letter's intention. He now carefully read each word.

Dear Will,

You will probably find this letter as difficult to read as I find it difficult to write.

Please know that I am sorry. I know this letter will hurt you. You can be certain sure that I love you, but we cannot be together. I will miss you.

I've gone to Kentucky to take a teaching position in an Amish school. Please do not try to come find me. I feel this is the best for both of us.

I can't explain everything because I don't have a lot of time, but I didn't want to leave without telling you goodbye.

I pray that you will find a nice *Englisch* woman to love and that the two of you will have a family that you can raise to know *Gott*.

This is not easy for me to do, but it is necessary. I hope you have a happy life without me.

Always,
Your Sally

P.S. There is some good news that I wanted to tell you too. My family will be able to keep the farm after all! Isn't that wonderful gut?

William refused to cry as he reread the words in disbelief. Sally was gone? How? Why? None of this made any sense! This wasn't true, was it? It was a joke. A very bad joke. It had to be. Sally wouldn't write this letter. She loved him. She wouldn't just leave him for no reason.

He stared out at the house. Did Sally's mother or sisters hold the answers? Will blew out a breath and killed the engine. He wasn't just going to leave without inquiring why Sally had left. He couldn't.

He marched to the house and knocked on the door. A woman, who William recognized as Sally's mother, opened the door.

"Is Sally, uh, Saloma, here?"

Her mother shook her head. She looked out toward William's vehicle. "She said to give you the letter, and that it would explain everything."

Explain everything? "Why did she leave?" Will made his best attempt to keep his composure.

"She is going to be a teacher." Her mother's tone hinted at pride.

"But she had a job here."

"She won't be going to that job anymore."

William felt like shaking the woman. How could she be so nonchalant about her daughter's leaving? Didn't she realize that he'd just lost the love of his life? The one he'd been making plans with for a bright future together? The woman he'd hoped would take his hand in marriage and bear him children? The only one he longed to grow old with?

"When will she be coming back?" he asked in desperation. He could wait a year or two, couldn't he? Patience certainly wasn't his strongest virtue, but he could possess it if need be.

"She's not coming back. She will stay in Kentucky."

Will wanted to protest. There were a hundred questions he needed the answers to, but doing so would have cast suspicion on his and Sally's relationship. If he let on that they'd been involved romantically, there was no way on earth she'd ever be able to come back. He had to keep his head about him.

"I'd like to correspond with her. May I have her address? Uh, her employer will want to send her a thank you note."

"*Nee.*"

"No?" Will's jaw dropped.

"She said not to give the address to anyone."

"If I give you a letter, would you be able to send it to her for me?" Did he sound as desperate as he felt?

Saloma's mother shook her head. "I'm sorry." She moved to close the door. "Goodbye."

Will stared at the closed door just inches from his face. So that was it? No chance of communication with Sally? William's chin hung to his chest and he ambled back to his Jeep.

How was it that one day could be the best day of your life and the next day the worst? How was it that a person could feel such joy one day and the next day he could feel such pain? And how was it that Sally could profess her love one day and leave him alone and brokenhearted the next?

Uncle George had been right all along.

ELEVEN

Paloma knew she should be thrilled about her new teaching job; it was all she'd ever wanted to do since she was a little girl, but, somewhere along the way, the position had lost its glittering appeal. As she read through the latest edition of *Blackboard Bulletin*, she found herself longing for Will.

But a life with him could never be.

Sally brushed away the tears that relentlessly cascaded down her cheeks. Leaving Will had certainly been the most difficult thing she'd ever had to do, but she couldn't see any viable alternative.

Every time she imagined Will reading her letter, it felt as though someone had thrust a sword through her heart. She knew he loved her, and she hated the fact that she was hurting him. Did he know her heart was breaking too? Did he notice the tear stains on the letter she'd left for him?

If only there was a way.

Someday, in the distant future, this would all make sense, but, for now, Sally couldn't fathom why their reality had to be so brutally heartbreaking.

Lord, please heal our broken hearts. Mend them with Your perfect peace and love. I don't understand what it is, God, but You have a plan in all this. Help me to trust You. Help us both to trust You.

Saloma took a cleansing breath and placed her *kapp* over the tight bun at the nape of her neck. She didn't know if she could get through her first day of teaching without breaking down in tears, but she would try.

She thought of Will. He had his college classes to attend. Would either of them be able to focus on their tasks at hand? Saloma doubted it.

No, she was quite certain life would never be the same for either of them again.

"William, is everything all right?" Uncle George walked into the library where William had been studying.

He pressed his palms to his eyes, attempting to dispel his tears of frustration, and regarded Uncle George. "No. Everything is *not* all right."

Uncle George walked to William and squeezed his shoulder lightly. "Want to talk about it?"

Will was taken aback by his uncle's gentle voice. His normal tone was usually more strained.

William lifted his hands. "I don't understand what happened. Sally and I were getting along great. I even bought her a ring! How could she just leave me?"

"I'm truly sorry, William."

"You were right all along. How did you know?"

"I've seen it before. I've talked to those on both sides. It just seems that the Amish are too different from us." Uncle George rubbed the stubble on his chin. "Think about it. Can you imagine living your entire life without electricity? Without reliable transportation, having to depend on others to take you into just the next city? Their whole thought process is different. Most of them don't even vote."

Will shrugged and realized it was true, although he didn't want to. He had been blind to their differences, believing that somehow they could overcome them. They could've compromised on the things they disagreed on, couldn't they? Life together wasn't completely impossible, was it?

"Why would she leave?" Will couldn't help his pleading tone.

"Give me a man who can understand women and I'll give you a million dollars."

Was his uncle attempting to lift his spirits? Will did appreciate it. He'd been desperate for a father figure since his father passed away, and, although he knew that Uncle George could never truly fill that void, he appreciated his attempts.

William locked eyes with his uncle. "Thank you, Uncle George."

"Please come to me any time. I'm willing to listen and offer the best advice I can give."

"I'm grateful for it." Will nodded, and then watched his uncle slip out of the library and into his office.

TWELVE

"Saloma Troyer?"

Saloma glanced up from her desk. Deep in thought, she'd forgotten she was waiting on a ride.

"I'm Elam Zook. Bishop Hershberger sent me to give you a ride."

Saloma smiled at the handsome young Amish man. "*Gut* to meet you. Elam was my *vatter's* name. I'll just be a minute." She turned to gather the papers that she'd been scoring.

"I can help with that." Elam moved to the desk and handed her one of the papers that had fallen onto the floor.

"*Denki.*"

Elam held her bag while she entered the buggy, then handed it to her. He quickly moved around the front, being sure to pet his driving mare, then slid into the seat beside her.

"So, you come from Pennsylvania?" Elam slightly adjusted his straw hat then made a kissing sound to signal the horse forward.

"*Jah.*"

"My folks are from Ohio. Moved down here a few years back 'cause the price of land is cheaper in these parts. I've heard it's pretty expensive in Pennsylvania too."

"That's what I've heard. I don't know much about real estate prices."

"When'd you get here?"

"Just a couple of days ago."

"*Jah*. We didn't have meeting last Sunday. It'll be this week at the Lengachers' place."

It would be a while before Saloma had a chance to meet everyone, but so far the folks she'd met seemed nice. Even so, she still missed home.

"We'll be having a singin' after the service too. I could drive ya home then if you'd like."

"That's a kind offer, Elam. I'm not sure what I'll be doing yet."

"You got a beau back home?"

The thought of Will tormented her soul. "*Nee.*" *Not anymore.*

"*Gut.* I mean, uh, there's quite a few single young men here. I don't know if you're interested."

"I'm not really looking," she said quietly.

"Ah, so you *did* have a beau back home. I see. That's okay. I still think you should come to the singin', though." He playfully nudged her shoulder with his. "I think you'd have fun."

"I'll think about it."

"Just don't wait too long. We lonesome fellas can't wait around forever." He winked.

Saloma laughed out loud for the first time in days, and it felt good. "Okay, I'll keep that in mind."

William had never realized how vulnerable love made a person, until Sally's departure. How on earth did she expect him to just forget about her, and move on with his life? He didn't want to forget her; he wanted to marry her.

What could be more important to her than their relationship? Was she really that eager to secure a teaching position? She said she loved him, so why would she leave? Had her mother or the bishop discovered their relationship and sent her away? Was that why she left? None of this situation made a lick of sense.

Desperation for answers sparked an idea. What if he traveled to Kentucky and visited all of the Amish schoolhouses? Finding them wouldn't be too difficult, would it? It certainly wouldn't be impossible. He could search the Internet for Amish communities there, and then ask around. Would the Amish folks tell an *Englischer* where their schoolhouses were located? It would be a task, for sure, but nothing was too difficult if it meant finding Sally.

He'd set out tomorrow as soon as the morning service ended.

THIRTEEN

Saloma closed her eyes as her hands deftly moved to wash the large serving dish. The church meeting here in her aunt's Kentucky Amish district had been a little different than what she was used to back in Lancaster County. The sermons seemed a bit shorter, and the ministers used more English than Bishop Mast or the ministers in her home community typically did.

It seemed there were many other differences in this community as well. Aside from the difference in dress and head coverings, the folks here were allowed to use bicycles for transportation, and their buggies were black and shaped differently, along with many other nuances she would have to get used to. How long would it be before the leaders here required her to change her dress and *kapp*?

She glanced out the kitchen window at the same time Elam turned. He spotted her quickly, smiled, and waved hello. Elam was indisputably attractive; she noticed a few girls look his way during the service, but her heart would always belong to Will. If only circumstances were different. Saloma sighed and quickly grabbed another dish and began washing it.

Aunt Fannie sidled up to her. "I'll wash up the rest of these dishes. You go ahead and go meet some of the young folk. Find Rebecca; she'll introduce you to some of her friends."

"*Denki*, Aunt Fannie." Saloma nodded and searched the room for her cousin. "I don't see her."

"*Ach*, I think she may be out yonder." Aunt Fannie tiptoed and peered out the window. She pointed to a quilt under one of the trees in the yard.

Saloma quickly found her cousin, but was reluctant to walk up to the group of young ladies. She proceeded with caution.

"Saloma," Rebecca beckoned, "*kumm*, sit by me."

Saloma did as bidden.

Rebecca smiled. "We were just talking about you."

Saloma felt her cheeks darkening.

"Don't worry; it wasn't bad. Mary was asking if y'all were gonna come to the singin' tonight," the teen girl next to her cousin on the quilt said. "I'm Patricia."

"*Gut* to meet you, Patricia." Saloma smiled. "I haven't decided whether I'm coming tonight or not."

Another girl leaned closer, her voice soft. "Well, if ya don't, my brother will be awfully disappointed."

Saloma's eyes widened. "Your brother?"

"Elam. He's mentioned your name more than once since you arrived." The girl cast a knowing smile.

"Mary! You shouldn't tell her that," Patricia chided the girl.

"I'm not looking for a beau," Saloma stated. Her heart ached every time she thought of Will. What was he doing now?

"Why ever not? Don't ya wanna get hitched?" Mary's jaw dropped.

"*Nee.* I'm not ready yet."

The girls looked at each other and suddenly, with understanding eyes, nodded.

"I still think you should come to the singing," Rebecca said. "You don't have to ride home with anybody."

"Yeah, it'll be a lot more fun than sittin' at home," Patricia agreed.

"I'll think about it." Saloma took a deep breath and glanced toward the house. Handsome Elam caught her eye and, again, smiled. She smiled back politely.

William drove along the dark backroads of the Kentucky countryside. He should have made reservations at a motel, but hadn't been thinking clearly when he'd left Pennsylvania. He only had one thing on his mind: finding Sally. Now, his cell phone didn't have reception.

He rounded the corner and noticed a buggy approaching. *Sally!* He flashed the lights of his Jeep and flipped a U-turn behind them. He flashed his lights again, but the buggy kept moving. *Why won't they stop?* He pulled up beside the vehicle, and leaned over and cranked the window open.

"Sally?" he called out.

A teen girl leaned forward and the young man in the buggy shook his head.

"I'm sorry," William said.

The young man nodded and urged his horse forward.

William turned the Jeep around again and continued the way he was originally headed. *I should have asked them where a motel was!* he chided himself.

A mile down the road, another buggy approached. He immediately slowed down and flashed his lights again. Hopefully, he could find his way to a motel. There was no telling how far out in the boonies he was.

"Excuse me," he hollered out the window before the buggy could pass by. The buggy came to an abrupt halt.

"*Jah?*" a young Amish man answered.

"I'm lost." William pulled to the road's shoulder, and quickly crossed over to the buggy on foot. "Do you think you could point me in the direction of the nearest hotel?"

"*Ach.*"

William heard a woman's voice and glanced to the passenger's side. "Sally?"

She looked up and William nearly fell over.

"Will? What are you doing out here?" her voice sounded shaky.

The young Amish man studied Sally. He spoke some words in Pennsylvania Dutch that Will didn't understand.

Sally nodded.

"Sally, I need to talk to you," Will pleaded. He wished the two of them had a language only *they* could understand.

"I told you not to come looking for me," Sally said.

William glanced again at the young Amish man. "Do you mind if we talk for a minute?"

The young man held up both his hands. "Go ahead, Saloma, if you want to." He said a few more words in their native tongue, and briefly touched Sally's hand.

William frowned at the intimate gesture. Who was this guy?

Sally looked to the Amish man, nodded, and exited the buggy.

Will led her across the road, and they stood in front of his Jeep. He wanted to take her in his arms, but refrained from doing so. It seemed the guy in the buggy was watching them like a hawk. "I've missed you so much, Sally. Why did you leave?" He couldn't help the emotion in his voice.

"I had to. We're not a good match, Will."

"That's not true, and you know it! We love each other. We can make it work." He reached up and rubbed her arms.

"Will, don't do this! It's hard enough as it is." Tears shimmered in her eyes.

"Why? Why is it hard?"

"You can't understand."

"I might if you tell me. Did I say something? Did I do something wrong?"

Tears trailed her cheeks and she shook her head. "*Nee.* You did everything right."

"Well, then, what's the problem? You're not making any sense. At least give me a good reason."

"You're *Englisch* and I'm Amish."

"That's not a good reason."

"I don't know what else to say."

"How about the truth?"

Sally glanced at the buggy. "I have to go."

"No. Sally, please don't!" He desperately pulled her close and pressed his lips to hers. He tasted the salty tears that made their way to her lips.

She pushed back forcefully. "No, Will! We can't."

Will felt a firm hand grasp on his arm and glanced into the young Amish man's sober face. "Take your hands off my girl," he demanded.

"*Your* girl?" Will's brow lowered in confusion, and he looked at Sally.

Sally nodded. "That's right. *Denki*, Elam."

Will stumbled back in shock. "Sally?" His eyes searched hers.

"I'm sorry, Will. Please. Just forget about me and move on with your life. Goodbye."

Just forget? How on earth could he just forget?

He watched in consternation as Sally walked back to the buggy, hand-in-hand with the young Amish man named Elam. How could she just find another boyfriend in the short time they'd been apart? Could this really be happening? Had he really lost Sally?

It's true. Sally's not coming back. Ever.

As the buggy wheels turned, Will couldn't help but cling to his vehicle's door and cry aloud. He vowed then and there to never trust another woman again.

Sally thought that facing Will would be the hardest thing she'd ever have to deal with, but hearing his cry echoing in the darkness would surely follow her for the rest of her life. Would it be any easier if Will knew the truth? She didn't think so.

No, the truth would only hurt even more.

FOURTEEN

$\mathscr{P}$aloma had been quiet for the remainder of their buggy ride. She brushed away the tears, hoping Elam didn't see them. Pain exploded in her chest, and it felt as though someone had stacked an entire library of books on top of her. Every breath came with effort. She wondered if she and Will would ever be able to love another again. Right now, loving anyone the way she loved Will seemed unfathomable, and the thought of never seeing him again was excruciating. Oh, how she'd miss him!

"So, that was him?" Elam finally spoke, his voice compassionate. He turned the buggy down the country lane where Aunt Fannie lived.

"*Jah.*"

"I know it's none of my business, but why did you break up, other than the fact that he's *Englisch*?"

"I…I'm not ready to talk about it yet." She sucked in a sob.

"I understand." He brought the buggy to a stop. Elam's hand gently rubbed the top of hers. "Listen, Saloma. Whenever you're ready to talk, I'm willing to listen. And I won't tell anyone."

"*Denki*, Elam. You're a kind man."

His brow lifted slightly, accentuating his azure eyes. "I hope we can be friends."

"*Jah*, I'd like that." If she were in search of another sweetheart, Elam would surely be a good match. But, at this moment, a romantic relationship with anyone seemed impossible.

"Goodnight, Saloma."

She exited the buggy then watched until the flashing lights of Elam's rig were out of sight. Save a few stars in the sky, darkness haunted this wretched night. She lifted her face to the heavens and closed her eyes, a slight breeze caressing her face. *Please help us through this, God. This is so, so hard. I don't know how to move on without him, Lord, but I know I have to. I wish it didn't have to hurt so much. Please take our pain and help us both to live again.*

The two hours of fitful sleep he'd received didn't give Will the rest he desired or needed. He glanced at the alarm clock and determined it would still be a few hours before daylight appeared. He grabbed the extra pillow, and shoved it under his head and stared up at the ceiling in the dark. Echoes down the hallway told him that not everyone in this motel had sleep in mind. If he planned to drive back to Uncle George's place first thing in the morning, he'd better get some shut eye.

Thoughts of Sally were torture enough, notwithstanding his unsettling dreams. What could they have meant? He cast his anxious thoughts aside, buried his head under the blanket, and determined to find some rest. Tomorrow would be a long, lonely day.

The Amish woman in the motel lobby had to be a sign. He had to at least try to talk to Sally one more time before he left town.

"Excuse me, ma'am. Do you know where the nearest Amish schoolhouse is?"

The woman eyed him warily.

"I'm looking for Saloma. She's the new schoolteacher from Pennsylvania."

The woman nodded in recognition. She gave Will directions, which he quickly wrote down on the closest thing available – a motel napkin.

"Thank you." He reached for one of the cinnamon rolls provided as part of the motel's continental breakfast. He looked at the Amish woman. "Did you make this?"

She nodded demurely.

"It's the best I've ever had." He quickly grabbed a couple of napkins and a cup of coffee, and hurried out the door.

Twenty minutes later, he arrived at his destination. School children played all around and barely seemed to notice him. He strode into the schoolroom to see Sally hunched over the teacher's desk.

"Hey, beautiful."

"Will! *Ach*, what are you doing here?"

"I had to talk to you before I left."

"School will start in just a little while. I don't have a lot of time."

"Just answer one question for me. Why did you leave?"

"Will, I'm not supposed to say anything."

"What do you mean, you're not *supposed* to say anything? Who told you to keep quiet, and why would you listen to them?"

She shook her head.

"Sally, please. I *need* some answers." He raked his hand through his hair. "I cannot just walk away from the woman I love, without a reason!"

Tears shot to Sally's eyes. "Will, please don't do this! It's hard enough."

"How do you think *I* feel? At least you have answers. I'm in the dark here. Please, Sally, how do you expect me to leave you forever for no apparent reason?"

"Not forever. We will both be in Heaven, *ain't so?*"

"Yes, that's true. But, who's to say we can't work through this? Sally, love and faith can conquer anything." He took her hands in his.

"I told you. I have Elam now," her voice shook. She pulled her hands away.

"Baloney! Do you think I believe that for one second? You don't make a good liar, Sally."

Her cheeks reddened. "I told you that I cannot say anything. If he finds–" Sally abruptly stopped. "I've already said too much."

"Who's *he*? The bishop?" Will searched her eyes to find the answer. "Do you mean my Uncle George?"

She didn't need to say a word. He had his answer. Yes, this is exactly something that his uncle might do. He'd been against Will and Sally's union from day one. "What did he do? Did he threaten you?"

"No, Will."

"What did he say to you?"

Sally frowned.

"Never mind. I'll make him give me the answers." He looked out the window at his Jeep and determined his next move. He reached for Sally's hand. "Please, Sally, wait for me. Don't give up on us yet. I'm going to do everything in my power to make it work between us. Please don't give your heart to anyone else."

She shook her head. "Will–"

He placed his fingers over her lips. "I know you think it's impossible. God will make a way. I'm sure of it. Our God moves mountains, Sally. He works things out that seem impossible. Have faith, sweetheart."

"You don't understand."

"No. *You* don't understand. With God *all things* are possible." He leaned across the desk and kissed her cheek. "Next time I come back here, I'm taking you as my bride. Goodbye, my sweet Sally."

Sally wanted to break down in tears. If Will only knew that it really was impossible. She was quite certain that even God would not intervene this time. Could He turn back the hands of time? Will would surely be devastated when he found out the truth – a secret kept for years.

An undeniable secret.

FIFTEEN

$\mathcal{B}$y the time Will reached his uncle's estate, he was livid. And determined. And desperate for answers.

He tore in to the circular drive, thrust the gear shift into park, and screeched to a halt. He stormed into the mansion and sought out his uncle. A twist and jerk of the handle on Uncle George's office door, with no result, reminded him that his uncle's office was off-limits. He pounded on the door.

"Uncle George, are you in there?" his shout echoed through the house.

The house was quiet. Where was Uncle George?

He moved to check the library, the den, and then scrambled up the spiral staircase in search of his uncle, but he was nowhere to be found.

"William?"

He leaned over the balustrade and frowned at his uncle.

"What is all this ruckus?"

William careened down the staircase, like a bulldozer plunging full-speed into a mound of dirt. "I demand you tell me what happened! Why did Sally leave, and what do you have to do with it?" His temperature escalated with each word.

Uncle George answered calmly, "If I gave you an answer for that, you wouldn't like it, William. It's better if you don't know. You should just move on with your life."

"No. I'm not stepping aside. I want answers!"

Uncle George expelled a heavy sigh. "*I can't. I promised* your parents."

My parents? "What do my parents have to do with this?"

"I've already said too much." He walked to his office door. "I'm sorry, William. I'm not at liberty to say."

"Please. I need answers." Will's throat became dry, and he felt tears of frustration threatening once again.

"It's for your own protection. Please, just forget about all this, and move on with your life. It's for the best." He shook his head and stared a hole into the floor. "How I wish you'd never met that girl."

Will's jaw went slack. He heard the lock turn on his uncle's office door. Once again, he'd been locked out from the answers he so desperately wanted, so desperately needed.

Will attempted to listen to the professor's words, but he could only hear the thoughts in his head. At this rate, he may as well just quit school. It certainly wasn't doing him any good.

How would he make a good counselor for someone else if he couldn't even deal with his own issues? Was this God's way of letting him experience what his future clients would be going through?

All he knew was that this was painful. He wanted answers, and it frustrated him to no end that those with the answers wouldn't share them. What did Uncle George mean by 'it's for your own protection'? What did he need to be protected from? Was his life in danger somehow? Were his parents part of the Mafia, or something?

Another thought crossed his mind. Was Sally's life in danger too? Is that why Uncle George sent her away? Had he led the enemies to her doorstep by showing up in Kentucky? He thought carefully about what she'd said. Did she leave any clues that her life might be in danger? She'd said 'he' couldn't find out, but Will assumed she'd been referring to Uncle George. Maybe someone else had threatened her...the person who was trying to take their house, perhaps?

Will felt like pounding his head into the table in front of him. How could he protect Sally if he had no clue what was going on? Did he even know what was going on?

One thing he did know for sure – he *would* find the answers.

SIXTEEN

Will took in his surroundings as he walked to his Jeep. He hadn't noticed anyone suspicious. He made sure to check his rearview mirrors to be certain he wasn't being followed. With his wild imagination, he couldn't help but be a little paranoid. However, if someone wanted to take him out, wouldn't they have done it already?

He pulled into the circular drive and jogged to the house. Maybe he should have parked in the garage this time. He hoped Uncle George would be home. He made sure to lock the door behind him, just in case someone had foul play in mind.

"Uncle George, are you here?" He knew the chances of his uncle being home in the middle of the day were slim, but nothing seemed to be normal lately.

Marita peered around the kitchen corner. "Your uncle said he was stepping out for a few minutes, sir."

"So, he *was* home?"

"Been home all day."

This was indeed odd. "Thanks, Marita."

As he walked down the hallway toward his bedroom, he noticed something peculiar. Was Uncle George's office door open? For the entire year-and-a-half since his father passed away and he'd moved in with Uncle George, not once had his uncle's office door been left open. Strange indeed. He glanced around to see if anyone was lurking nearby.

Will dashed to his bedroom and tossed his backpack on his bed, then hurried back to Uncle George's office. He quickly closed the door behind him and moved to his uncle's desk. He sifted through paper after paper until he noticed one particular document. It was the deed to Sally's home.

He carefully read over the words, until his eyes stopped cold on one name. His own. *What on earth?*

Now he was really confused.

He didn't even notice the door handle twisting. "What are you doing in my office?" alarm clearly marked his uncle's voice.

"What is this, Uncle George? Why is my name on this paper?"

His uncle grimaced. "William, you shouldn't be in here."

Will jerked up from his uncle's office chair. "Answer my question! Why is *my* name on *these* documents?"

"I guess there's no sense keeping this from you, as you're determined to find out at any cost." Uncle George shrugged, then sighed. "You are the rightful owner of the Troyer property, William."

"The rightful own– I don't understand." He frowned.

"Have a seat. This isn't going to be an easy pill for you to swallow."

He crossed his arms and stood his ground. "What do you mean?"

"The answers you've been searching for. Please, William, just sit down."

"Did you steal their property?" His voice rose an octave.

"Steal their property? Of course, not." Uncle George took a deep breath. "William," his uncle locked eyes with him and spoke slowly, "Elam Troyer was your biological father."

Elam Troyer? It took a few seconds to comprehend his uncle's words.

An earthquake couldn't have shaken him more. This wasn't true. It couldn't be. *God, this can't be true.*

"My...father?" He shook his head. "You're lying! My father is...was Peter Griffith."

"I'm sorry, son."

"Why would you fabricate all this? Did the Mafia put you up to this?"

"Mafia?" Uncle George frowned. "William, I don't think you understand. Those are documents your parents drew up. There is no Mafia involved."

Will shook his head in disbelief. "You really do hate Sally, don't you? I can't believe you would go to this length just to keep us apart!"

"William, I am telling you the truth, as God as my witness. Your mother was married to Elam Troyer before she met your adoptive father. It didn't work out between them. I don't think she ever told Elam about you."

Will felt as though a large vacuum had sucked all of the air out of the room. "Why should I believe you? How can I believe this is true?"

"Because it is." Uncle George shrugged. "Denying this is not going to make it any easier for you, William."

"So, *if* this is true, that means that Sally is my...my sister?" William swallowed and felt the bile rising in his throat. He suddenly felt sick. He rushed to the restroom and emptied what little contents were in his stomach. *No! I cannot be in love with my sister!*

"William, are you all right?" his uncle called from the other side of the bathroom door.

"No, I'm *not* all right! I'm in love with my *sister*! So, now what? What are Sally and I supposed to do?" *Great! I finally find someone I want to spend the rest of my life with and now this? How is this fair, God?* Was this some sort of generational curse? None of this made any sense at all. "This is just a nightmare, right? None of this is true. It can't be."

"I'm sorry, William, but it is *all* true. Saloma Troyer would be...is...your half-sister."

William stepped out from the bathroom and closed the door behind him. He still felt weak, so he sank down onto the library's couch. "Did you know this the entire time? Is this why you were so against me dating Sally?"

"No, I wasn't aware of the fact until a colleague brought the case to my attention. That's when I realized that your girl-friend's troubles were one and the same. I realized right away the gravity of the situation and the potential danger you were in. That's why I sent Saloma Troyer away."

"So it wasn't the Mafia! *You* sent her away."

"What choice did I have?" He shook his head. "And where on earth did this whole Mafia thing come from?"

"Never mind," Will mumbled.

He stared at his uncle and swallowed hard. "So, does she… does she know?"

"I'm afraid so. That's why she agreed to move away." Uncle George sighed again. "I'm sorry, William. Now you can see why I'm not too keen on the Amish."

"What do you mean? What did Sally ever do to you?"

"Not her. Elam Troyer. You don't understand how devastating it was for your mother when your biological father left. She cried every day for weeks. I don't think any of us knew how to comfort her. I certainly didn't. She didn't realize that she was pregnant with you at the time; otherwise, I'm sure she would have begged him to stay."

Will stared at his hands. "Why *did* he leave?"

"I have some of your mother's belongings. I suppose this would be an appropriate time to give them to you." He walked into his office, removed a key from his top desk drawer, and opened up a locked mahogany filing cabinet. He pulled out a thick folder and handed it to Will. "I think this might explain things a little better."

Will took the file folder, but didn't dare look inside. No, he wasn't ready yet. He needed time to process the blow he'd just been dealt.

If what Uncle George was saying was indeed true, then his whole life would change. Not only would *Sally* be his sister, but he'd have seven other sisters and a stepmother – all Amish. The thought was dizzying and, in a way, a little fascinating. He'd pretty much grown up as an only child, so the thought of having siblings intrigued him.

Just not Sally. Why, of all the people in the world, did it have to be Sally?

Could he *ever* see Sally as a sister after their intimate relationship? Now, he was so thankful they'd never gone beyond much more than kissing. And even that thought was disturbing, in light of their incomprehensible reality. How would he be able to get her out of his mind and heart? How would he ever be able to see her as just a sister?

Sally was absolutely right. Their situation was truly impossible.

SEVENTEEN

"I'm curious about something, Uncle George. How did my father's will come about? I mean, that's not usually something the Amish do, is it?"

"Some do, some don't. Kind of like the *Englisch*." He shrugged. "I was already studying law at the time, and I suggested it. I had a friend draw it up for them, although I didn't know what all it entailed at the time. It seemed pretty standard, though. Each one agreed to leave their worldly possessions to the other. Your mother eventually changed hers to include Peter instead."

"But Elam – my father – never did?"

"Not that I know of."

"Do you think it's wrong that he didn't change it? His possessions should rightly go to his Amish family, not me."

"I think he should have *included* them, yes. But, as a man, he should be responsible for *all* his offspring. Under normal circumstances, the property would most likely be sold, and the sale of the estate would be divided among the deceased's survivors. Since the will was between *your* parents, the will only pertains to you. You have the legal right to possess the property, if that is what you wish to do."

"I could never make them leave their home. I mean, they're my actual family. I have Amish family," Will said more to himself than his uncle. He shook his head. "This is all so strange."

"Indeed."

"So, what happens now?"

"That depends on you. They have a temporary lease on the property."

"We're making them lease? But–"

"As Executor of your mother and father's estate, I had to do what I felt was in your best interest. Don't worry, they're not paying a lot. When you turn twenty-five, you may do with the property as you wish. I hope that you won't do anything without first talking to a financial advisor about all your options."

"What options?"

"You could continue leasing the property to the Troyers."

Will began to protest, but his uncle continued.

"Now, don't say anything until you hear me out. Listen, William. I know they're your family and you want to do right by them, but there's a good chance the Troyers might not *want* to have anything to do with you. After all, you are a son from a previous marriage that – I'm not certain about this – but, according to my colleague, they knew nothing about. They might not even believe you are who we say you are. They might think you're just someone out to steal their property and take advantage of them. Not to mention, you're an *Englischer.* We have to approach this situation with caution."

Will had never considered that they might not want him around. Uncle George had a valid point.

"Your other options would be to move into the place yourself, rent it out, or sell it."

"But what about Sally's family, *my* family? I'm not just going to kick them out."

"We can help them relocate."

"How will they be able to afford land out here? It costs a fortune. I couldn't do that to them."

"William, I realize that you desire what's best for them, but you need to look out for your own interests as well. Think about it. Your father prepared the will because he wanted to be sure to provide for you."

"I thought you said he didn't know about me."

"True. But when he signed those papers, he was married to your mother. He knew very well that there was a good possibility they would have children someday. The will states that his possessions will go to his spouse, which is your mother, and any surviving children produced by their union. He wanted to provide for *you.*"

Will shook his head. "I know my legal rights, but I have to do what I feel is morally right. The fair thing would be dividing it up so that everyone gets a share, but I can't do that right now. I can't evict my family from their home."

Uncle George sighed. "I can't force your hand, William, but just consider how things might be ten years from now. You could be married and have a family of your own. Owning a nice farm might be something of interest to you. By then, the youngest siblings will have married and moved out. Who knows, your stepmother could remarry some widower and have more children. Then *he* would possess the home. It could cause even more problems down the road. I think you should take your chance while you have it. It'll be hard on them at first, but they'll adjust."

"I won't do that. I'd rather lose the house than kick them out onto the streets. For crying out loud, they just lost their father and husband! I couldn't do that to them."

"I understand. You don't need to do *anything* now. I think it would be in your best interest to continue with the lease agreement we've already made, then we can determine where you'd like to go from there. Does that suit you?"

Will nodded. "That's fine, I guess."

EIGHTEEN

George stared at the documents on his office desk. The task at hand would not be pleasant. As a matter of fact, he'd been putting it off for far too long, but he could put it off no longer. He would visit Elam Troyer's widow today.

When he sent Saloma away, he'd hoped he wouldn't ever need to return to that wretched farm. It conjured up too many unpleasant memories. A brisk wind blew leaves across the road and, with it, the last twenty-four years seemed to erase. His expensive luxury vehicle disappeared, and he was back in his pickup truck once again.

George stared over at Elam, who sat across the bench seat. A gentle breeze danced through the open windows and into the cab. "Do you know what you're doing, Elam?"

"Jah. I'm going home."

"No, you're not. Your home is with my sister – your wife!" George frowned at his one-time friend.

Elam stayed silent and that only caused George's blood to boil more.

"You're a coward, running back home to Mommy and Daddy."

Elam looked away. "You're Englisch; you can't understand."

"You're right, Elam. I can't understand why in the world you would want to leave your wife. Don't your people read the Good Book? Did you miss the part that says 'what God hath joined together, let man not put asunder'? Did you not read the passage where God says He hates divorce? How about the part that says 'Husbands, love your wives'?"

"Bishop Mast says worldly vows don't mean anything. They're not bound by the church. It's only the vows we make to the church that we have to keep."

"That's ridiculous! So you're telling me that you were lying through your teeth when you stood at the altar and married my sister? Is that what you're saying?"

"No. I married your sister because I thought I loved her."

"You thought you loved her?" *If George hadn't been driving, he certainly would have knocked Elam into next Tuesday.* "You have another woman, don't you? That's why you're leaving my sister, isn't it?"

"No, never!"

"I don't believe you."

Elam shrugged.

"You're despicable. You and all your kind. Don't you ever show your face around my sister again. You don't deserve her anyhow."

"I don't plan to."

"What is wrong with you people? You think that just because you're Amish you have some special connection to God? That you can just make up your own rules and ignore what He says in His Word? Well, that's where you're wrong. You people are about the furthest from God there is. A horse and buggy and plain clothes never saved anybody and never will. And it certainly doesn't make you live right." George wished that he could go back and erase the previous year for his sister's sake, and save her from a broken heart, but he knew that was impossible. Never in his life would he ever trust another Amish person again.

George had a whole lot more he could say, but what good would it do? Elam's mind had been made up. Both George and Elam stayed silent for the remainder of the ride to his parents' home.

George snapped out of his reverie and realized where he was. *This home. Which was now the home of the woman Elam had left my sister for.*

Will had been standing in front of the mirror for the last thirty minutes. Maybe he was not the best person to judge, but, by his estimation, he hadn't received one drop of Troyer blood. It might be easier to see Sally as a sister if they looked alike just a little bit, but he just couldn't see it.

He glanced down at his watch and realized that if he didn't take a shower soon, he would be late for his psychology class. Now that he knew the Mafia wasn't after him, and he'd learned the actual truth about Sally, maybe he'd be able to get through the rest of this semester and earn his degree.

Although he had a bazillion questions, he still hadn't plunged into his mother's belongings. That could wait. Life was too emotionally hectic right now for him to concentrate on too many things at once. And that meant focusing on school.

Now, if he could just get Sally out of his head...

With heavy hand and heart, George knocked on the door of the now-deceased Elam Troyer's home. Commotion from inside the home and a small face peering out the window indicated someone was present. George wiped a perspiring hand on the handkerchief inside his sport coat pocket.

The door slowly creaked open and a cautious woman stood, sober and silent. She nodded her greeting.

He must retain his professional demeanor, in spite of the animosity he felt. "Hello, ma'am. I'm George Anderson, Attorney at Law. I'm here to discuss the terms of your late husband's last will and testament."

The downtrodden woman nodded and eyed him curiously. "You are the one who came and spoke with Saloma."

"That's right, ma'am." He nodded. "And your name is?"

"Rosemary Troyer." She gestured to two hickory rocking chairs. "Would you like to sit on the porch?"

"Certainly, Rosemary." George hadn't expected the woman to let him into the home with no man around. That wasn't the Amish way.

She spoke a few words in Pennsylvania Dutch to two of her daughters, apparently in their teens. The girls nodded to their mother, then disappeared in haste.

George leveled his gaze at the woman. "I won't beat around the bush, Ms. Troyer. As you know, Elam Troyer left a will bequeathing all his earthly possessions, including *this* property, to his first wife and any offspring procreated by the two of them."

Rosemary nodded.

"This house and the property it sits on belongs to William Griffith, my nephew. William would also be your stepson."

"My...son?"

"By marriage, legally speaking. He *is* Elam Troyer's biological son."

"Then it is right that the property should go to his only son." Rosemary's countenance filled with anguish, and moisture gathered in her eyes. She quickly pulled a handkerchief from her apron pocket and dabbed her eyes. "I'm sorry. My husband…he…this was *all* a surprise to our family. I never knew he'd had another wife."

His colleague had been correct. "You were unaware that Elam was previously married?" George shook his head. How could Elam have been so insensitive? "He didn't even mention he'd been divorced?"

"*Nee.* I knew *nothing* of Elam's past marriage. When my family moved into this area twenty-two years ago, Elam was single. He was at the singing and clean-shaven, so I assumed he was available."

"Wait a minute. So, you hadn't been in the area prior to that time?"

"No."

"So, Elam didn't leave my sister for another woman," he said flatly. He'd been wrong.

"If he did, I can tell you that it was not me. I never even thought to ask whether he'd been married. Divorce is not something our people usually do."

"That's not what he told me when he left my sister." He clenched his fists. "You know, your husband and I used to be pretty good friends when we were younger. I never thought he'd turn out to be a–" George blew out a breath. "I'm sorry, but this whole situation has me so upset."

The front wooden screen door slammed shut, and Rosemary's daughters appeared with two trays – one with two glasses of refreshment and the other with an assortment of cookies and crackers.

Rosemary nodded. "Mr. Anderson, please have some tea and snacks."

"Obliged, ma'am." He took a glass of tea and one of the small plates, and nodded to the teen girls. "Thank you."

The girls quickly disappeared behind the screen door again.

"To think, he had a son all this time and never told me. It always wondered me why he didn't want me to open his mail. Perhaps that was why."

"I should probably clarify. As far as I know, Elam was unaware of William's existence. My sister didn't see any reason to tell Elam about his son. He'd left and moved on. Would a son have made any difference? If he didn't love my sister enough to stay with her, then I couldn't see a child changing his mind."

"I guess we'll never know." Rosemary's gaze leveled at George. "William's mother…does she know that Elam passed?"

"I apologize. I should have clarified that as well. No, William's mother passed away about five years ago. Both his mother and his adoptive father are deceased. William only has me and an aunt, whom he's never met, out in Arizona." He smiled briefly. "And now, he has your family as well."

Compassion welled in her eyes. "I am sorry for William. He has experienced a lot of grief in his young age."

George thought of William's relationship with Saloma. Yet another loss. "Yes, he has suffered much more than any young man should."

"How…how old is William?"

"He's almost twenty-four."

She nodded thoughtfully. "Elam and I were married for almost twenty-two years. We didn't court very long."

George guessed that was probably at the urging of their bishop. He would have wanted Elam to marry quickly, so as to have no chance of reconciliation with his former wife. The whole situation was sickening. And poor Rosemary, she was just an innocent bystander like his sister had been. "I'm sorry you had to end up with him."

"Please, I don't want you to think badly of Elam. He was a very *gut* father to my girls and husband to me."

"At least he was to someone," George mumbled.

"What will happen with the house? Should we prepare to move?" There was no hint of concern in Rosemary's voice, which surprised George.

"Do you have another place to go?"

"*Nee*. But I am sure we can find something."

"William and I haven't determined what will happen with the property. I'm Executor of his father's estate until William's twenty-fifth birthday. The lease you signed was temporary. If you're still agreeable to the lease for another six months, we can pursue that option if you'd like."

"When will I meet Elam's son?"

"I believe you already have. He's been picking up your daughter several times a week for some time now."

Rosemary's eyes broadened. "That was him? When he came to the door after Saloma left, I knew there was something about him that looked familiar, but I couldn't quite place my finger on it. Now I know. I saw Elam in his eyes."

"He does somewhat resemble Elam, but he's definitely got more of his mother in him." He set his drinking glass on the floor and rose from the rocker. "Well, I best be going now. It was a pleasure meeting you, Rosemary."

She nodded. "Will you bring William next time?"

George smiled. "I'll see if he'd like to come by and meet his new family."

As George traveled home, he was struck by a new perception. *William's Amish family isn't at all what I'd thought they'd be.* Instead of the unpleasant picture in his mind, he'd discovered Elam's family to be kind and compassionate. Just like William. *Imagine that!*

NINETEEN

Saloma rushed to her bedroom as soon as Rebecca informed her of the letter she'd received in the mail. She'd always liked to read her personal mail in a private setting and this was no exception. Especially since she already knew who it was from. *Will.* She'd been waiting for it, expecting it.

Her hand caressed the envelope, as though he were still holding it. She imagined his steady hand, heavy with grief and shaking slightly. Saloma brought the letter close to see if any of Will's scent, a drop of his cologne perhaps, had clung to the letter.

She turned the damper to raise the flame on the kerosene lamp, and took a deep breath before tearing into his letter. Her eyes hesitantly read the words as her heart silently cried for her lost love.

Dear Sally,

I don't know where to begin. I never thought I'd be writing a letter of this nature. This is all so heartbreaking and strange. My uncle recently informed me of what you already know – we have the same father. This is still a shock to me, as I'm sure it is to you too. To think we are brother and sister! Oh, how I wish it wasn't so! I don't know if I can ever see you as anything other than the love of my life. If only circumstances were different. If only there was a way.

I know that I said the next time I come to see you it would be to take you as my bride. Now I know that will never be. You were right. Our situation is impossible. With that being the case, I have something to say. I release you to court and love whomever you please. You have my blessing.

With a heavy heart,

Your brother, Will

Saloma folded the now-tearstained letter and placed it under her pillow. It was official. There was no hope for her and Will. Even *he* acknowledged it.

It was time. Will could wait no longer to reveal the contents in his mother's file.

He had no choice but to come to grips with his reality. The letter to Sally had been the most difficult of all. The anguish in his heart didn't negate the facts, no matter how much he longed for an alternative truth. Releasing Sally to love another had been excruciating, but isn't that the essence of real love? When you truly love someone, you desire the best for them. No matter if your own heart is breaking in two, yearning for what can never be.

Will turned to the task at hand. He sifted through all kinds of important papers. He lifted out his birth certificate. His eyes roamed the document until it came to the place of birth. *I wasn't born in Pennsylvania? That's odd.* He was pretty certain Elam and his mother lived in Lancaster County when they married. He searched the stack of papers on the table beside him, the ones he'd just waded through, and found his parents' marriage certificate. Sure enough, they'd married in Pennsylvania.

He frowned. He'd have to ask Uncle George about that later.

Will's gaze landed on something. He pulled out a leather journal and brought it to his nostrils. He'd always loved the smell of real leather. His hand caressed the book as though he were holding something sacred – and he felt that it was. As he opened the cover, his mother's penmanship immediately caught his eye. It was different than he remembered. *Hmm...it must have changed over the years.*

Sandra Anderson. He rarely heard his mother called by that name in his growing-up years; she'd always been Sandy, Sandy Griffith. It seemed strange to read her maiden name.

Will scanned most of the journal; he could read those parts later. What he was searching for was his own existence and that of his biological father's. As of now, he only had Uncle George's word and his father's alleged last will and testament. It wasn't that he didn't trust that his uncle was telling the truth, it was just that he needed more solid concrete evidence to *fully* believe his uncle's words. The fact that Uncle George didn't care for the Amish, and disliked Sally, made him suspect in Will's mind.

He noticed the dates in his mother's journal nearing the time of his birth, and he flipped back a couple of pages. The name 'Elam' written inside a heart jumped out at him. He read the words below it.

> I can no longer deny it. I'm in love with him. I've fought it for so long, but I can't deny it anymore. He loves me too. I know he does. He asked to meet me on Sunday night and I said yes.

> Tonight's the night. I have butterflies in my stomach and I wonder if he does too. If our parents knew, I'm certain they wouldn't allow it. Especially his – they are different than my folks. (I wonder if he'll kiss me.)

> Remember how I wrote that Elam was different than me? Well, I tell you why. He's Amish. He doesn't drive a car or anything, just a horse and buggy. He wears homemade clothes, just like in the olden days. He also wears suspenders and a hat that I think makes him look even more handsome. It brings out his gorgeous eyes.

> Yes! He loves me! He told me so tonight. I'm excited to follow our love to see where it leads. Could he be the one?

> we've been seeing each other every week now. I hope we never stop. I love him so much!

> Elam is all I ever dreamed of. He's kind and handsome. I hope he's the one.

> Tonight we talked about the future — you know, marriage and all that. He said that he loved me, but he seemed sad somehow. He said that if we married, he'd have to leave his family behind. I couldn't imagine leaving my family just because I want to get married to someone I love.

> Elam came in normal clothes tonight! I think maybe he's becoming used to the idea of becoming what he calls an 'Englischer'.

> He gave me a ring last night! He wants to marry me! You should have seen how sweet and shy he was about asking me. I could just picture him taking his money to the jewelry store and asking to look at rings. I love Elam so much I can hardly stand it! I'm so excited I don't know what to do. Our future is so bright.

> Well, today we did it. We went down to the courthouse and said 'I do'! I feel like the happiest woman alive.

> I love being married to Elam, he's the best husband ever!

> We haven't seen his folks or any of his family since we married. We might go visit them next week.

> Guess what? Elam received Christ today! I was so happy to see him walk to the altar and ask God to save him. Now I know we can get through anything.

> Well, tomorrow's the day we'll go see Elam's folks. I'm a little nervous.

> I don't know what's wrong. He seems so sad. He went to see his folks today, but they wouldn't even allow him to come onto the property. I fear they hate me. I hope Elam doesn't regret marrying me. I would never want to be a burden to him.

> We tried again today. We've gone several times now and it's always the same thing. We are not welcome.

> The Amish deacon came by today and spoke with Elam. He told me the man said he was officially shunned. Only repenting in front of the Amish church and joining again would lift the ban.

> Elam loves me, I know he does. But he's so, so sad for his family. It pains me to see him this way. Sometimes, when he thinks I'm asleep next to him, I hear him crying at night. I don't know what to do. I don't want to lose him.

> I didn't want to admit it, but now I have no choice. He misses his family too much. I fear it's more than he can bear. I think he'd rather be with them than me.

> They came again today, the Amish people. I wasn't in the room but I overheard. Some I didn't understand because they didn't speak it in English. They want him to leave me. I know it. They told him a piece of paper doesn't make someone married.

> I can see it in his eyes. He's leaving. He cried last night again when we were in bed. But it was different this time, he was weeping. He thought I was asleep, but how could I sleep when I see how much turmoil he's in? I want to be enough for him — I yearn to be enough for him, but I'm not. I realize that.

> Elam held me tight last night and told me that he loved me. I think that was his way of saying goodbye. I hope I am wrong. God, please let me be wrong.

> I'm letting him go. I feel he will be happier this way. We should have never married. I can see that now. I've only brought him pain and heartbreak.

> He's gone. That's all I can bear to write.

> I've never been so sad. I've never known such heartache. I don't know how I'll go on.

Will stopped reading and wiped his eyes. His mother's pain was so tangible, he felt as though it were his own. Just like she'd lost Elam, he'd lost Sally. He continued reading his mother's words.

> I have a secret...

A secret? Me? Was I her secret? Will raised a brow, and then continued.

> I'm going away. I will come back sometime. Maybe in a couple of years, I don't know. I think George knows my secret.

> I found a place. The people here are nice and there are others here like me, who are expecting, with no man around. I don't know their situations, but I'd guess no one's situation is like mine. I can never regret knowing Elam, but my heart hurts so much. I still wonder every day about what he's doing.

> I had it all planned out. I would have the baby and give it up, but now I cannot bring myself to do that. He's perfect. I've decided I'm keeping him.

> Although he'll always be a reminder of a love that never should have been — no, that is not true. How could it be, when I hold this precious little one in my arms? I love him so much, even though, when I look into his eyes, I see his father. Little William. He is my consolation, my gift from God.

> I've thought about going back home. I miss my parents and brother.

> There might be a way. I've met a very kind man. We got to talking, and it turns out that he is a preacher and he said he knows my brother, George. What a small world! He adores little William.

And me too, it seems. I cannot bring myself to love him, though. The pain in my heart is too deep still.

> He wants to marry me. I'm not sure how I feel about that. I'm scared and thrilled at the same time. What if he leaves me, like William's father did? But what if he doesn't? He wants to adopt William and call him his own. I'm unsure of what I want.

> I'm going back home! He said everything will work out just fine. I want to believe him. He said God will see us through. He's a really good man. I've decided to marry him. His name is Peter.

> My parents really like him and, of course, George does too. They love our baby too! I'm happy.

> He is a wonderful father to William. I'm sure just as good as William's biological father would have been. Sometimes I wonder where he is and what he's doing.

> Peter has been the best husband, yet I'm still afraid to love him. I don't know if I can ever give him all my heart. I've done that before...

> I've decided not to tell William about his biological father; it would only bring him pain. I have no reason to tell him anyway. He has a fine father now.

> William is growing so big and strong now. He has Elam's eyes, I think.

> He wants to grow up to be just like Daddy, he said. I smiled, because I think he has the best daddy in the world.

> I thought my heart would stop today. I saw him. We passed each other in the grocery store. He immediately looked away. I had william with me. He was with an expecting woman and a little girl who looked to be a few years younger than william. I wondered if he recognized his own son. I'm guessing the woman was his new wife. I hope he is happy with her. I really mean it.

> I'm so in love I can't stand it! And I have another secret. william doesn't know yet, but his daddy and I are going to have a sibling for him to play with by the end of the year. His father and I are thrilled.

> We lost little christopher last night. He was really sick. We will have a funeral for him in a couple of days.

> I don't think we will try to have more children. Losing the ones you love is too painful. But I'm so glad for young william, and of course, Peter, my beloved.

Will didn't need to read any more. Not today. He'd found what he'd been looking for. It was there in black and white. Uncle George had been correct all along. He wasn't just making this up to keep him and Sally apart. Any thread of hope he held out for a relationship with Sally had slipped through his fingers.

His mother was so right. Losing those you love was painful. Will felt closer to his mother somehow; reading her words made him realize how alike they were. He could identify with his mother in a way he never had when she'd been alive. His heart grieved for his mother and the fact that she, behind her cheerful appearance, had been a soul cloaked in sadness. He guessed that she'd probably carried it around every day since Elam had left.

But hadn't she said that *he* was her comfort?

Will smiled. He'd never realized how much joy he'd brought his parents. If only he could go back to when they were still alive, and thank them for all the sacrifices they'd made for him over the years. If only he could tell them what a blessing they'd been to him. But that would have to wait until Heaven.

Will felt a sense of loss as he thought about the father he'd never had a chance to know. He must've been a decent man, otherwise his mother wouldn't have married him. Would she?

Another thought struck him. His mother wrote that Elam had accepted Christ. That meant he *would* indeed meet the father he never knew, in Heaven!

TWENTY

Saloma grasped the chalkboard eraser and began removing the children's assignments she'd previously outlined. A feeling of accomplishment satisfied her soul as she thought of little Ruthie Borntreger. She'd done well with her English lessons today, something they'd been working on for nearly a month now.

"Ready?"

She turned, and her shining eyes met Elam's.

"Good day today, huh?" His brow rose.

"*Jah*. Ruthie's doing much better. I think I'm finally getting through to her."

"That's great. You need any help?"

"I've got it." Saloma put one of her teaching books into her tote bag and strolled toward the exit.

"Want to stop at Yoder's and get an ice cream?" Elam picked up the reins and set the buggy in motion.

Saloma bit her lip. Although she and Elam weren't 'officially' courting, it seemed they were pretty close to it. He'd asked to court her but Saloma couldn't bring herself to say yes. Letting go of Will had been the most difficult thing she'd had to face, but even more difficult was the realization that they had absolutely no chance of ever getting back together.

"Saloma?"

"*Ach*, sorry. I was daydreaming. Ice cream would be wonderful, Elam." She may as well agree to court Elam. He was everything any Amish girl could want – hardworking, kind, and handsome.

Elam adjusted his hat to block the sun. "Thinking about your *Englisch* beau again?"

She shrugged. "*Jah*. And us."

"Us?"

Saloma nodded.

"I like the sound of that." He grinned. "But I think there are things we need to talk about, ain't so? You never did tell me why the two of you broke up."

"*Nee*, I didn't. I wasn't ready."

"Are you ready now?"

She dipped her head and took a deep breath. "It is kind of a long story." Saloma went on to explain how she met Will, the revelation she'd learned afterward, and everything that had happened since. Talking about it helped to sort out her feelings, and she found she became freer with every word she spoke. "So, I basically discovered I was in love with my brother."

"Well, I'd say that's a good reason to break up!" He scratched his head. "Now that's not something you hear every day. Wow! Your brother."

"I know. What would have happened if we'd never found out, and ended up marrying?"

"I don't know. I guess it was better that you found out now. So, what about the house then? What will happen with it?"

"I'm uncertain yet. I can't see Will making *Mamm* and my *schweschdern* move, but I'm not sure about his uncle. He doesn't take a liking to Amish folks."

"He wouldn't be the first."

"*Nee.*"

The atmosphere in the buggy became silent, and Saloma waited for Elam to speak the words she was sure both of them were thinking.

He studied her thoughtfully. "So, where does that leave us?"

"Free to court, if that's what you'd like."

Elam's smile broadened. "I'd like it very much."

Saloma smiled back at Elam. The truth was, *he* seemed more like a brother to her than Will did.

Will looked at his uncle. "Was that all you had of my mother's belongings?" He yearned to know more. How did his mother and father meet? What did her parents think about the two of them dating? What did *his* parents think? Were they still alive? Could he possibly still have living grandparents?

"I'm afraid so, William. Your mother didn't leave much."

"But I have so many questions."

"Like what? Perhaps I can answer some of them for you."

"Well, how did my parents meet?"

"Are you referring to your mother and Elam Troyer, or Peter?"

"Elam, my biological father."

"They met at a mud sale. Elam was running a booth for his mother. She had quilts and dolls, those sort of things. Your mom used to love things like that," he mused aloud. "Anyway, I think they were immediately attracted to each other. They struck up a conversation, and your mother said that she felt like she'd known him her whole life."

"Then what happened?"

"Well, she must have given him her contact information because, next thing we knew, a buggy showed up at the house. And continued about twice a week for some time. The more time they spent together, the more in love they became. Eventually, they married."

"I don't understand why it didn't work out."

"They seemed to do just fine until his Amish community became involved. You see, he was already a baptized member of the church. And marrying your *Englisch* mother meant he'd be shunned. I don't think he counted the cost before he stepped out of the church. They sent him letter after letter, some loving and some downright mean. Then they started coming in person. They told him he would surely go to hell."

"Just because he left the Amish?"

"Yes, because he had forsaken the vow he made to the church and disobeyed his parents. Becoming *Englisch* to the Amish is like choosing a life of sin, or worldliness, as they call it. They believe that, since God placed them in an Amish home, it is God's will that they stay and follow the Amish traditions."

"That's ludicrous! I knew that their salvation included works, but I had no idea to what extent."

"Not *all* Amish believe that way, but I'd say most do."

"So, he left because of the pressure?"

"That may have been part of it, but I think he went back because he missed it. For the Amish, family and community are everything. They do everything together. Can you imagine having a dozen or so brothers and sisters, not to mention all the cousins, aunts, uncles, and friends? It is very difficult for a person who's grown up in the Amish culture to leave it behind."

"I can imagine. So, he chose them over Mom and me."

"Over your mother, yes. He didn't know about you, remember?"

"Poor Mom."

"She didn't want him to go, but she saw how miserable he was. She let him go because she loved him, but I know her heart broke in two. And then she found out about you."

"She originally planned to give me up for adoption, right?"

"Yes. She didn't feel like she was adequate to raise you alone. But, as soon as she saw you, she changed her mind. She knew there was no one on earth who would love you as much as she did. I think she was right." Uncle George grinned.

"How did she meet Dad?"

"Peter was my best friend. I thought he'd be a good match for my sister and a good father to you." He smiled. "I was correct." Will smiled.

Uncle George continued, "When your mother went to the unwed mothers' home to have you, Peter was just finishing up seminary. He was interested in counseling, like you, and I suggested that he volunteer at the home where your mother was staying. They'd met before, but never had a chance to get to know each other. I don't even think your mom remembered him. He knew your mother's situation. Right away, his heart went out to her. When they got to know each other better, they both discovered what I'd thought all along – that they were perfect for each other. Of course, it was very difficult for your mother to open her heart again after what Elam had done."

"I can imagine."

Will had gained a new respect for his uncle. He'd thought Uncle George was against him, but all along he'd just been trying to protect him. Will attempted to swallow the lump in his throat. "I'm sorry, Uncle George."

"Sorry?" His brow arched.

"I've been a jerk lately."

Uncle George chuckled. "Oh? I hadn't noticed."

"Please forgive me."

"There's nothing to forgive. It's easy to become frustrated or misjudge when we don't understand the circumstances."

"Even so, I've been disrespectful when I should have been thankful. I don't know where I'd be if you hadn't taken me in after Mom and Dad passed away. Thank you."

"I'm confident you would have been just fine." His uncle squeezed his shoulder. "But I wanted you here. This house gets lonely sometimes. You've almost been like a son to me. I'd like to think that if I'd ever had a boy, I would've wanted him to be like you."

"Why did you never marry, Uncle George?"

"I had a girlfriend or two when I was younger." He shrugged. "I guess I just became married to my school, and then to my job. Families take a lot of time and effort to maintain. I didn't think I was cut out for that type of responsibility. Of course, that doesn't mean I've never longed for a family."

"I think you would have made a fine husband and father."

Uncle George smiled. "I'm just glad I have you, William."

Emotion built in Will's throat. "I'm glad I have you too."

TWENTY-ONE

*"W*ould you like to meet your stepmother and sisters today?" Uncle George peered over the morning newspaper.

Will finished the bite of omelet he'd just taken, and set his fork down. "Sure."

"You look reticent."

"Well, I'm not sure how they're going to accept me, that's all."

"I think they'll love you." His uncle smiled. "You don't have anything to worry about."

Will took a sip of his orange juice.

"William, did her family know the two of you had been dating?"

"No. Sally was too afraid to tell her mother that she was dating an *Englischer*. She didn't want her to put a stop to it."

"It's probably just better if they don't know, don't you think?"

Will shrugged. "Well, there's no point in saying anything now."

"I agree. No need to add more stress to an already-stressful situation." Uncle George exhaled a relieved sigh.

"When do you want to go?"

"After breakfast."

Will nodded, and his stomach turned a somersault.

As Will and Uncle George pulled up to the Troyer residence, Will noticed his stepmother and the girls in the garden. "One, two, three, four, five, six, seven. I think every one of my sisters is out there."

"All but one," his uncle corrected.

Will sighed. "Yeah." Of course, Sally wasn't present. Part of him wished she was, the other was glad she wasn't. Seeing Sally would be too difficult.

"Ready?" His uncle shut off the engine.

"Yep. Let's do this." Will rubbed his hands together.

They walked silently into the yard, and Rosemary stood from her crouched position and wiped her hands on her apron. She spoke something in Pennsylvania Dutch and each of the girls went and stood by their mother.

Uncle George spoke first. "Rosemary, I'd like you to meet your stepson, William."

Emotion rose in Will's throat, but he caught himself. He held out his hand to his stepmother. "Nice to meet you."

She hesitantly shook his hand and eyed him curiously. She nodded. "You *are* Elam's son."

Did she see some of his father in him? Will wanted to ask. It was a pity the Amish didn't keep pictures of loved ones. He would have loved to see what his father looked like. He hadn't seen one in his mother's things. He'd have to ask Uncle George later. Perhaps he kept one somewhere.

"Yes, he is," Uncle George concurred.

"These are your sisters: Clara, Lucinda, Rosy, Mary, Katy, Judy, Becky, and you already know Saloma," Rosemary introduced the seemingly-shy girls.

Will wondered what each of them were thinking.

The girls stared shamelessly. One of the girls whispered something in Pennsylvania Dutch to another one, and she giggled.

"What's so funny?" Will smiled.

"My sister said you're too handsome to be our brother," the girl divulged. Her sister, who had spoken the words, turned three shades of pink and nudged her sister.

Perhaps they weren't as shy as he'd thought. Will's eyes sparkled in amusement. "Well, I think you all are much too pretty to be *my* sisters."

Rosemary said something again in their native tongue, and the three oldest girls disappeared into the house.

Will swallowed. "I'm sorry for your loss. How did Elam, uh, my father, die, if you don't mind me asking?"

"He had a bad heart."

"Oh." Will put a hand to his own heart and briefly pondered if his condition was hereditary. "So, it was a heart attack?"

She nodded.

"Can William see the house?" Uncle George spoke up.

Her eyes widened briefly, then she nodded.

"It can wait," Will interjected. "We can sit out here and talk for a while."

Rosemary led the way to the front steps and spoke to the younger girls, again in Pennsylvania Dutch. The girls quickly gathered folding chairs and brought them to the porch.

Will sat on one of the chairs.

"How long has the home been in the Troyer family?" George asked.

"Elam's grandfather built this home."

Will frowned. He'd rather get to know his family than details about the home. He didn't want it to seem like he was there just because he was interested in the property. "Are any of Elam's parents or grandparents still living?"

"*Jah.* They live with his brother, his *grosseldre* do."

"Are they here in Lancaster County?"

"Near Lititz."

"That's north of here, right?"

Rosemary nodded.

"I'd like to meet them sometime. Are his parents alive too?"

"His *mamm, jah.*"

"Does she live in Lititz too?"

"With Elam's sister."

"How many brothers and sisters does Elam have?"

"He has three sisters and five brothers. One of his sisters lives here in Paradise, the other two in Lititz. His brothers all live in Lititz as well."

"Wow! It looks like I'm going to be busy getting to know everybody."

"Elam would have been happy to know he had a son."

Will swallowed hard. "Do you really think so?"

"For sure and for certain."

"I wish I could have met him." Will glanced at Uncle George, who frowned. "Although, I had a great adoptive father, thanks to my uncle."

The older girls returned and Lucinda, the second oldest one, Will supposed, timidly offered Will a whoopie pie and juice. He smiled and grabbed a whoopie pie from one of the small plates.

"They are all for you," she said.

"*Three* for *me*?" His jaw lowered. "Uh, okay. Thank you." He smiled and took the plate with the other two pastries. His gaze moved to Uncle George, who nodded with an amused smile.

Rosemary said something to the girl.

"Would you like some *milch* too?"

"Milk? Sure. Thanks." Will studied Uncle George. He didn't appear to be surprised at all. Of course, he'd had plenty of interaction with the Amish in the past. Will had virtually been kept away from Amish culture his entire life, it seemed. He guessed it wasn't by accident.

The others also took snacks and the girls joined them on the porch.

"Are you all in school?"

"Just Mary, Katy, Judy, and Becky. We are finished," Clara, the oldest one said, gesturing to Lucinda and Rosy.

Will's brow shot up. These girls looked too young to be out of school. "What are your ages?"

Rosemary pointed to each of the girls. "Clara's seventeen, she'd the oldest after Saloma, then there's Lucinda, she's sixteen, Rosy's fourteen, Mary is thirteen, Katy and Judy, the twins, are ten, and Becky is eight."

Will studied the girls more closely. He hadn't even noticed the girls were twins. They must not have been identical twins. "I probably won't be able to remember all your ages, so you may have to remind me later."

Becky, the youngest, looked at her mother and whispered something.

"*Jah*, Becky," Rosemary said. She looked at Will. "She said you remind her of her father."

His eyes sparkled. "Oh? How's that?"

Becky shrugged. She whispered to her mother again and Rosemary encouraged her to speak aloud. "You are kind."

"You think so?"

The girl nodded.

"Tell me what you're learning in school right now," Will coaxed.

"She doesn't speak English too *gut* yet," Katy volunteered.

"Oh, so you're learning English?" He smiled at Becky.

Becky nodded.

Will looked around at the other girls. "How about the rest of you? Do you like school?"

"I'm almost done!" Mary proclaimed.

"You still have another year," Judy reminded her sister.

"Mary wants to be a teacher," Katy said.

Will smiled. "That's wonderful. I want to be a kind of teacher too. A counselor."

"That's what Mose Brenneman is," Becky said.

"No, silly. Mose is a carpenter." Lucinda laughed.

"What is a counselor?" Mary asked.

Will enjoyed getting to know his sisters. He wondered what it would have been like growing up with them. "It's someone to talk to about problems and get advice from."

"Kind of like a friend?" Clara asked.

"A friend that gets paid," Uncle George chimed in.

"You're going to be paid for being someone's friend?" Lucinda's eyes widened.

"It's different than just being a friend," Will explained. "A counselor goes through years of school and training. We have to learn human behavioral patterns and how to best deal with specific issues. Like marriage problems."

"Are you married?" Clara asked.

"Well, no."

"How can you give other people advice on marriage if you ain't never been hitched?" Rosy asked.

Uncle George chuckled.

"The Bible is the best marriage handbook there is. That's where I'd find my answers." Will smiled. "And I do hope to be married…someday, Lord willing."

The girls looked at each other and smiled.

"You must be real smart," Rosy said.

"William is an intelligent young man, you can be sure of that," Uncle George agreed, his chest puffed out a little.

Will shook his head and changed the subject. "Who made these delicious whoopie pies?"

Pink momentarily stained Clara's cheeks.

"They're wonderful. Is this one strawberry?"

Clara nodded.

Will looked at his uncle. "We need to get the recipe for these so Marita can make some for us."

Uncle George agreed with a grin.

Will briefly wondered if his attitude toward the Amish had changed any since their visit. He'd have to ask him about it later.

"Is Marita your *fraa*?" Lucinda asked. "Your wife."

Uncle George chuckled. "No. I'm not married. Marita is my employee. She cooks for us and cleans the house."

"Oh. We cook and clean too, but we don't get paid." Rosy frowned.

"If you're good at it, you can get a job doing those things for other people," his uncle suggested.

"*Jah*. But *Mamm* needs help here. 'Specially since *Dat* died," Mary said.

"Is there anything I can do?" Will volunteered.

He felt his uncle's disapproving stare heavy upon him. "You have your studies," he reminded.

"I'm aware of that, Uncle George. I *do* have some free time as well."

"We could use help harvesting the corn," Clara said.

"When? What would you need me to do?"

"You'll have to hitch up the team first," Clara explained.

"The horses?" Will frowned. "Someone might have to show me how to do that."

"Well, John Yoder can come over and hitch up the team for ya." Her cheeks darkened.

"She likes John, but John likes Saloma," Rosy said.

"Rosy! *Nee*," Clara scolded her chatty sister.

Will's brow shot up. "Saloma?"

"*Jah*. But Clara's hoping he'll ask to court her now that Saloma's gone." Rosy continued, "Besides, Saloma has Elam now."

"Rosy," Rosemary warned. She spoke a few words in Pennsylvania Dutch, directed at the girl.

Just the thought of Sally with someone else jerked Will's heart. But he couldn't think of her the same way – he mustn't. *She's my sister*, he reminded himself.

"How is she doing?" he asked.

"*Gut*," Lucinda said. "She likes teaching, but I think she misses home."

I miss you too, Sally. Oh, how I miss you!

TWENTY-TWO

W scanned the pages of his mother's journal in search of clues to the past. He wished she'd written more about his biological father. He desired to know more about this man. Was he like his father in any way? Did he inherit any of his father's traits, other than his eyes, and apparently, his kindness? The latter part gave him a sense of pride. It was indeed a blessing to have a goodly heritage.

He stopped cold when the words leaped off the page.

> Received a letter from William's father today, but I refuse to read it. My life is perfect now and I feel the contents could possibly upset that somehow. I forgave Elam for leaving long ago, but I do not wish to open old wounds. I will save it. Perhaps William will want to read it someday.

A letter? He frantically began searching through the file Uncle George had given him. He hadn't seen a letter anywhere. Had Uncle George removed it? He carefully sifted through each document, but came up empty. Where could it be?

He sprang from his bed and headed toward the den.

"Uncle George, do you know anything about a letter?"

His uncle removed his glasses and pinched the bridge of his nose. "Letter?"

"Yeah, from my father, Elam." He thrust his mother's journal in front of his uncle.

Uncle George returned his glasses to the perch on his nose and read where Will's finger pointed. He shook his head. "I'm sorry, William. I don't recall seeing a letter among your mother's things."

"How about a photograph? Didn't my parents at least take wedding photos?"

"I don't know, William. Your father had been Amish. There's a good chance they didn't take any together. At least, I don't remember ever seeing one."

Will felt like pulling his hair out. Couldn't he just have one photo of his father? Just one.

"But she said that she saved the letter for me. If it's not in the file, then where would it be?"

"If I knew, I'd tell you."

"Are you sure this is all we have of my mother's belongings?"

"We donated her other things to charity, remember? Peter kept the important items. As far as I know, you have it all now."

Will sighed in defeat. "Okay. I just thought that maybe..."

Will yearned to have a piece of his father. What would it have been like to grow up with Elam Troyer as his dad? He'd most likely have learned more physical skills. Would he be a farmer right now? A carpenter? He couldn't help but imagine how it would have been if his parents had stayed together and raised him.

Of course, he would never regret having Peter Griffith as a father. Peter had taught him the ways of the Lord, leading by example. As the son of a preacher, Will wished his father had been home more often than he was. But Will understood that other people were counting on his father too.

If Elam had raised him, there would be a good chance that the two of them would have worked side by side every day. And, although Elam had left the Amish, Will realized he probably would have kept many of their customs and traditions. As it turned out, though, Elam kept all their traditions. Even if it meant leaving his mother alone to rejoin his Amish group. He briefly wondered if his parents ever discussed the possibility of his mother becoming Amish.

But, then, if his parents had stayed together, then Sally and her sisters wouldn't exist. It was peculiar how God wrought a unique tapestry from all their mismatched threads. Will wondered what it would look like when He was finished.

Saloma took her latest letter from her sister Clara and tucked it into her apron pocket. She'd already read it, but desired to read it again to savor every word. As she walked down the secluded country lane, she thought of home. Being around her cousins wasn't the same as being with *Mamm* and her sisters, and she sorely missed their fellowship.

She thought of the words Clara had written. To think Will had been inside her home! Well, his home. She wondered what he'd thought about the place. He'd only ever been outside in his Jeep to pick her up for work or one of their dates. How she missed spending time with Will. She now wondered if they'd ever be able to have a brother-sister relationship. The fact that her sisters had opportunities to be around him provoked envy.

Her sisters had all loved him, as she assumed they would. She could feel Clara's subdued excitement as she wrote about Will, their 'new *Englisch* brother', she'd called him. She mentioned that he'd complimented her whoopie pies. All of the girls were pretty good at baking, but it seemed Clara had always had a natural knack for making things taste delicious.

Picturing her mother, sisters, and Will sitting around the supper table made her long for home all the more. What would happen if she returned home? Would seeing Will be too difficult? Over time, they'd get used to a familial relationship, wouldn't they?

But what about the deal she'd made with Will's uncle? Would he hold her to it? *She* hadn't been the one to reveal the truth to Will, his uncle had. And now that Will knew that he owned the property and that he was part of the family, he surely wouldn't make their mother and sisters move. Saloma was certain of it.

TWENTY-THREE

W]ll sat at the desk in his uncle's library, attempting to concentrate on his studies. He glanced up at his uncle, who sat on the sofa reading the daily newspaper. He looked back down at his text book, scribbled a few sentences in his notebook and sighed. This wasn't working at all. Maybe he should take the remainder of the semester off and re-enroll when he could focus better. There was no way he would pass his exams if he didn't get some clarity.

"Is something wrong, William?" Uncle George must've perceived his meandering thoughts.

"This is frustrating. I realize that Sally and I are related, and nothing can ever become of us, romantically speaking. What I can't understand is why on earth I can't get her out of my head."

"William, just because your circumstances have changed that doesn't mean your feelings will automatically change as well. You know in your head that you must let her go, but your heart doesn't want to. It is like breaking up with a girlfriend. You think and dream about what could have been, but you know there's no chance of getting back together. But, in your case, getting back together with Sally is not simply unlikely, it is impossible."

"But how do I get her off my mind?"

"Read your Bible. Focus on your studies."

"I've tried all that. Nothing works. I'm thinking of taking some time off."

"From school?" Uncle George folded his newspaper and set it down beside him.

Will nodded.

"But you're almost done." Alarm creased his uncle's brow.

"I don't know how I'll ever get through this semester if I can't concentrate on my coursework."

"Why don't you start dating other women?"

Will adamantly shook his head. "No. I can't do that. It wouldn't be fair to the girl."

"Who knows? Maybe you'll fall in love."

"I'm not ready for that."

"What about a project?"

"A project? What do you mean?"

"Why don't you and I build something?"

Will grimaced. "I don't know if I'd be good at something like that."

Uncle George laughed. "Neither do I, but that wouldn't be the point. It would be something to occupy both of our minds, something out of the ordinary that would challenge our normal skills. I think it would be good for us."

Will shrugged and lifted a brief smile. "I guess it couldn't hurt. What will we build?"

"I'll let you decide."

"We could build a gazebo."

"Uh, that's pretty ambitious. For our *first* project, why don't we start out with something a bit more simplistic?"

"How about a picnic table? We could give it to the Troyers if it turns out."

"We're trying to get your mind off Sally, remember?"

"Yeah, you're right."

"I think a picnic table would go nice in the backyard."

Will nodded. "And if we enjoy making it, maybe we can build other things too. I think a couple of park benches would look great in the yard. Don't you?"

Uncle George nodded and smiled. "William and George, the carpenters."

"Sounds good to me." Will laughed.

Will perused the lumber, trying to decide which would be best to use for a picnic table. He noticed an Amish man looking at the lumber as well. *Maybe he'd know.*

"Excuse me, may I ask your advice?"

The man nodded.

"I'm building a picnic table and I have no idea what to use."

The man smiled. "Redwood makes a nice picnic table. Or you can use cedar or pine. Pine would probably be your most economical choice."

"I should probably use pine then, just in case I mess it up," William chuckled.

"What kind of picnic table are you making? Just a standard rectangular table or a fancy octagon?"

Will shrugged. "I hadn't really thought about different styles."

"Those fancy octagon tables sure do look nice."

"We'll probably just keep it simple. I'm not too handy with power tools just yet."

"I see." The man tipped his hat. "Well, then, God be with ya."

"Thank you."

Ten minutes later, Will overheard the same Amish man conversing with the cashier.

"Hello, Amos! How are you doing?"

"Hi, Minister Fisher." The cashier shook the man's hand. "Rosabelle and I are doing great."

"How are the little ones?"

"*Gut. Gut.*"

Will attempted not to listen to every word, although one thing did catch his attention. The man he'd been talking to was an Amish minister. Perhaps he could help Will with some of the questions that had been racing through his mind.

He quickly paid for his purchases, then hurried out the door in hopes of catching the minister. "Excuse me," Will called out, "but I overheard that you're a minister. Do you mind if I ask you a question about the Bible?"

The man finished loading the lumber in the back of his work buggy and offered Will his undivided attention. "Not at all. I love discussing the Bible!"

"Okay, the Bible says that nothing is impossible with God, right? And that with God all things are possible? But practically speaking, can God really work out impossible situations?"

"First of all, what we are asking of God must align with His will. God isn't a puppet. However, I believe that if we love God and are truly seeking His will and following His Word, that He wants to grant our requests. Think about this verse: *Delight thyself also in the Lord and he shall give thee the desires of thine heart.* The 'also' refers to the verse before it, which says *Trust in the Lord, and do good.* The way I see it, that can mean one of two things. Either God will give you what you desire if you delight and trust in Him, or He will place *His* desires in your heart so that your desires and His are one and the same."

"Wow, I've never thought of it that way."

"He also said that the Father delights in giving His children good gifts. But God sees the future; in fact, He sees the entire picture. He knows what is best for us. He knows what we need and what we don't need. We often think that we know what we want or need. I think that's because we're following our heart or feelings. How many people have followed the path of their heart's desire, only to find that it leads to heartbreak? God's ways are not our ways."

"I don't think I even got your name. Are you an angel or something?"

The man laughed out loud. "Wait until my Susie hears what you said! She probably won't believe me." He chuckled. "Or Bishop Hostettler, he'll love that one." He shook his head and the light caused a sparkle in his eye. "No. I'm Jonathan. Jonathan Fisher."

"That sounds familiar. I'm William."

"About your impossible question – let me ask you something." Will nodded.

"Can God bring dead bones to life? Can God defeat one hundred and twenty thousand men with an army of just three hundred? Can God open up the sea and let His people walk through on dry ground? Can God make the sun stand still? Can God make this beautiful world by nothing other than His voice? Can He make the blind to see?" Jonathan placed a hand on Will's shoulder. "Yes, God can work out the impossible, William. And He will, *if* it is His will."

"Do you know Saloma Troyer?"

"I believe she belongs to Bishop Mast's group, ain't so?"

"Yeah, I think so."

"No, I don't know the Troyers too well. Didn't Elam Troyer pass away just recently?"

"About six months ago, I believe." Will frowned. "He was actually my father."

"*Your* father?"

"Yeah, I just recently found out too. That's kind of what my question was about. See, Saloma Troyer and I were dating. I had in mind to marry her when I learned that she and I are actually half-siblings."

"Ouch."

"I know. So, that was my impossible question."

"That's definitely a tough one, I'd say. Who knows, though? God's done some pretty miraculous things. He can make a way where there is no way, just like He did for the Israelites in the wilderness." He shrugged. "Pray about it. The worst God can say is no, right?"

"I guess." Will sighed. "Listen, thanks, Jonathan."

"You're welcome. Just remember that God knows best and He has a plan for your life. Sometimes it's difficult to accept what we don't understand." Jonathan lifted a half smile. "I'll say a prayer for you too, William."

"I'd appreciate that."

"It was *gut* meeting you." Jonathan touched the brim of his straw hat and nodded as Will watched him drive off in his buggy.

Will couldn't help but feel this meeting had been orchestrated by God.

TWENTY-FOUR

Saloma raised her voice in song with the other young folks at the Singing. She glanced across the table, and Elam caught her eye and winked. His enthusiasm confirmed his excitement for the evening ahead. While Saloma enjoyed their buggy rides immensely, she felt like she was just using Elam as a distraction.

She sighed. Elam was too good to just be a distraction...for anybody.

Elam must've noticed her musing, because he'd stopped singing. When she realized he had, she looked up and he nodded toward the barn door. Usually, they'd stay and chat with the others and enjoy snacks. Would others talk if they left early together?

Two minutes later, she met him outside by the other end of the barn, where the horses were hitched. He'd already begun hitching up the buggy.

Saloma could still hear the others singing inside the barn. She wouldn't mind staying, but there was no use if she had no mind to participate.

"Saloma?"

She cocked her head at the sound of Elam's voice.

"Would you like to take a walk before we go?"

"*Jah*, Elam. That sounds *gut*."

Elam left the horse tied to the hitching post and came alongside Saloma.

"Let's walk along the pasture." Elam held out his palm, seeking permission to take her hand. Saloma nodded and quietly placed her hand in his.

"It's a nice night, *jah*?"

Elam smiled. "The weather is nice, *jah*, but I don't care to talk about it."

Saloma had suspected he had something on his mind this evening. She was right.

He stopped in mid-stride and turned to her. "I want to talk about us." His finger gently outlined her jaw. "Saloma, do you see a future...with me?"

She swallowed hard. "I...I..." Honestly, she didn't know what to say.

Elam stepped close, his gaze simmering with desire. "You're everything I've ever wanted."

Saloma wanted to speak, to say something, when Elam's lips lowered onto hers. His kiss was soft and filled with emotion, but...

"Elam," – she broke away – "I'm sorry. I'm not ready."

He nodded in understanding. "I'll wait for you, Saloma. It doesn't matter how long it takes you to get over him. I'm willing to wait."

A breeze came up, and she shivered slightly.

Elam quickly slipped his jacket off and placed it around her shoulders. "Is that better?"

She nodded.

"Come on. Let's get you home."

"*Denki* for understanding, Elam."

He shook his head. "You're a fine woman, Saloma. Any man would be blessed to have you as an *aldi*...or a *fraa*."

Any man except Will.

Will quickly buttoned his navy dress shirt and tucked the tails into his trousers. He grabbed his Bible and keys from the small dresser near his bed and headed to the dining room.

His uncle glanced up as he sipped his coffee.

"Uncle George, won't you come to church with me this morning?"

"No, thank you."

"Why?"

He frowned. "I have my reasons."

"Will you never tell me what they are?"

"It's complicated."

"Is there somebody at church you're trying to avoid? Because, if that's the case, there are other churches you can attend."

"William, you're going to be late if you don't leave soon."

"My dad was your best friend, right?"

Uncle George nodded.

"And he was a preacher."

"That's correct."

"But his best friend won't attend church? How does that make sense?"

"I have my grievances."

Now he was getting somewhere! "With God?"

His uncle sighed. "I'd rather not discuss this."

"But it's important. I want to make sense out of all this. How can I when you won't even tell me what's wrong?"

"This doesn't concern you, William."

"Of course, it does. You're my uncle. I care about you. I love you."

Tears pricked his uncle's eyes – something Will had never seen. "Sometimes I wish I had the faith your father had. He was a strong man."

Will nodded.

"Do you know when I last attended church?"

Will shook his head. "I just know I was young."

"It was about a year after your brother died. I guess you can say I lost faith."

"Because of my brother's death?"

"That was part of it, for sure." Uncle George sucked in a breath. "William, do you know *how* your brother died?"

"He got sick, right?"

"He was perfectly healthy. Your mother had taken him to the doctor for his well-baby checkup, where he received his vaccinations. She brought him home and he became fussy. His fever started to climb, so your mother called the doctor's office. They told her to give him some children's fever medication, and she did as they'd recommended. Nothing helped. She tried giving him a bath to bring his fever down, tried to keep him hydrated. Poor little Christopher screamed; he was in obvious pain. There was nothing we could do. He died the next day."

"Do you think the shots killed him?"

"There's no doubt in my mind." He scowled. "Your poor mother. She'd already been through so much. She didn't deserve to have to suffer this too. I wanted to find answers for her. I wanted to somehow make things right."

"What did you do?"

"I'm a lawyer. I did what any good lawyer would do. I wanted justice. I researched for months, questioned others who'd had children injured or had died in the same manner. I found out the ugly truth. These kind of reactions aren't as rare as they claim."

"But I thought immunizations are supposed to protect you from disease."

"In theory. And I'm not saying all vaccines are bad. The concept in itself isn't necessarily evil, and I don't believe the doctors are either. You can't blame them. They're just trying to make a living like the rest of us. It's how they go about manufacturing the vaccines. Some of them contain mercury, aluminum, and formaldehyde. Do you have any idea how dangerous these are to the human body?"

"Not really, but I've heard they aren't good."

"Well, to make a long story short, we went to court and lost, although the evidence I presented was irrefutable. I don't know what I was thinking, going up against a multi-billion dollar pharmaceutical company. I guess I thought there might be some justice in the world still. How wrong I was."

"I never knew all this."

"We didn't see any point in telling you. Besides, you were too young to understand at the time."

"So that's why you stopped going to church?"

"Tell me something, William. If God is so big and all powerful, why didn't He protect your brother? Why did He make your mother go through all that heartbreak, especially after what Elam did to her? Why didn't He, at the very least, let us win the case?"

"I don't know."

"Yeah, that's what I thought."

"But I do know that we can trust God. I do know that someday God will bring justice and judgement on the evildoers. I know that the Bible says that God is angry with the wicked every day. And I know that God loves you. And me. And He loved Christopher and Mom just as much. Who can know the mind of God? Nobody can. But I know that I'd much rather trust Him than live my life for the devil and add to the wickedness of this world.

"Like you said, there's already too much evil in the world. Everything we do affects someone else, whether we realize it or not. What we need to ask ourselves is do we want to influence others for good or evil? Do I want to complain about all that's evil in the world, or will I do my best to show others the love God has for them?

"The way I see it is it's like a movie. We are only watching one scene out of hundreds, or thousands even, but the power goes off before we have a chance to see the end. We see one little part and complain that the movie doesn't make sense or it was over before it ended. We don't see the part where the blind man finally sees. We don't see the underprivileged child rising above his circumstances to become the world's next genius. But God, He sees the whole entire thing, and He knows how it ends. And He promises that it will work out well for those who love and trust Him. He promises that it will be worth it all. The question is, do we trust Him? Do we believe that He will do what He says He will do?"

Uncle George placed a hand on Will's shoulder. "You make me proud, William. And I'm certain your father would be proud too. You will make a fine counselor."

Will waited.

Uncle George sighed. "You're right. I've been putting the blame where it shouldn't be. I just...I feel like such a failure."

Will's eyes widened. "You, Uncle George? I've never seen a more successful person. Just because you lost the case doesn't mean it was your fault. You tried your best, didn't you?"

"You bet I did."

"Then there was nothing more you could have done." He lightly touched his uncle's forearm. "You need to give this to God. Let Him handle it."

Uncle George nodded.

"May I pray with you?" Will didn't know how his uncle would react. They'd never prayed together before.

"Sure."

TWENTY-FIVE

"I have a request."

Uncle George cocked a brow. "Yes, William?"

"May we invite my Amish family over for Thanksgiving dinner?"

His uncle's mouth turned down, and he rubbed his forehead. "Do you *really* want to?"

"I think it would be great." Will smiled.

Uncle George sighed. "If it makes you happy, William." His gaze pierced Will's. "Will you invite Saloma?"

Will had been considering this very thing. It would certainly be difficult to see Sally, but he was resigned to God's will, whatever that may be for them. And since a romantic relationship was impossible, they were eventually going to have to come to terms with being siblings.

"Yes, I'd like to invite Sally."

"Are you sure, William? It'll be difficult for you to see her."

Will nodded. "I'm aware of that fact, but I also know that we will have to face each other sooner or later."

"Very well. I will inform Marita."

"Thanks, Uncle George." Will smiled.

Saloma folded Will's letter and sighed.

"Between you and me, I think you should go."

She stared into Elam's eyes. "You...you would *want* me to go?"

"Saloma, the sooner you get over him, the quicker I can have your heart. Yes, go."

Saloma shook her head. "But what if..."

"It can only be a good thing. It's not like you're going to kiss your brother or anything."

"You're right. And I miss my family so much."

"Just don't miss them so much that you stay there. I want you to come back to me." He gently tilted her chin toward him and searched her eyes. "Okay?"

She swallowed. Was he going to kiss her? "Okay."

Elam lightly caressed her cheek then dropped his hand. "*Gut.* I'll be waiting for you, Saloma Troyer."

Dear Will,

I appreciate your invitation to Thanksgiving dinner, however, I'm unsure if I may attend. Please ask your uncle if this is okay. I guess I can tell you now. Your uncle and I made an agreement that I would move away and not return to see you. I also was not to say anything about us being siblings — a fact that your uncle informed me of. In exchange for my agreement to his request, he agreed to let my mother and sisters stay in the house. I thought this was a good agreement, especially since finding out that we are related. Now that you know, there is no secret. But I don't want my mamm and sisters to lose the house because of me returning home. If you could talk to your uncle to be certain it is okay, I would appreciate it.

    Goodbye,

    Sally

Will hastily wrote back to Sally.

Dear Sally,

    Don't worry about Uncle George, he is different now. I can assure you that your mother and sisters will not lose their home. Please come.

    Will

George scribbled notes as he scrolled down the page of his computer – research for his current case. He normally didn't take cases unless he was confident he could win them. And he had won the majority of them, all except the one that *really* mattered. But William was correct, he'd been nursing his wounds entirely too long and it was time to let go of the bitterness he harbored in his heart.

He sighed and reverently bowed his head. *Okay, Lord. You can have this. Please free me from this guilt, this weight that has sat on my shoulders for what seems like forever. Help me to be the father figure William needs.*

As he lifted his head, he remembered the letter William had asked about. He walked to his confidential file and unlocked it. His sister's file wasn't the only thing he'd kept in this cabinet; he'd also kept the documents from Christopher's case.

He lifted the file and thumbed through it. Tears pricked his eyes, then began to flow freely. *I'm sorry, Christopher. I'm sorry I wasn't able to vindicate your death. I failed you and your mother. I should have fought harder. Please forgive me.*

"Christopher is with Me now."

George's head snapped up like a jack-in-the-box. Where had the words come from? He glanced around his office. *What on earth?* He was certain he'd heard a voice, clear as day.

"God, are you speaking to me?" George looked up, as though he'd be able to see Heaven.

Silence.

He sighed and placed the file back into the cabinet. That's when he noticed it. He reached into the drawer and pulled out a lone envelope that lay hidden under the other file folders. *This has to be it.*

George stared at the handwriting – his sister's. For William, it read.

Thank you, God. He breathed the silent prayer and jumped from his seat.

"William! William!" he called down the hall.

Will's bedroom door opened and he emerged in his plaid lounge pants and a t-shirt. He wiped his eyes. "What is it?"

George glanced down at his watch. Five thirty. "Sorry, to wake you, son. But I found it."

Will shook his head, obviously still on the verge of awakening. "Found what?" He yawned.

"The letter, I think. I'm not sure, but it's in your mother's handwriting and your name is on it. I didn't open it."

"Just a minute." George watched as Will disappeared into the bathroom and returned a moment later. His face looked like he'd just stuck it under the faucet, although he'd dried most of the water. "Now I'm awake."

George smiled. "Good. Open it."

"Why do you seem so excited about this? Is there something in here I don't know about?"

He shook his head. "I have absolutely no idea what's in there, but I have a good feeling about it. I've been praying." He grinned.

"Okay." Will shrugged, then eyed his uncle curiously. "You've been *praying?*"

George nodded in satisfaction. "Yes, you can say God and I had a little chat."

Will's brow raised.

"It doesn't matter. Just get on with the letter. Aren't you at all curious?"

Will took a deep breath and eyed his uncle, who seemed just as curious as he was. Honestly, he'd rather open his letter in the privacy of his own bedroom, but he didn't want to disappoint his uncle.

"Let's sit in the library," he suggested.

Uncle George turned his head. "You know what? I think I'll have Marita make us some coffee."

Will nodded and watched his uncle disappear from the room.

He looked down at the envelope in his hands and noted his mother's now-familiar handwriting. Would its contents help him move on with his life, or would it bring more disappointment?

He plopped down onto the library's sofa and reached for the pen on the small table adjacent to it. Will slid the pen under the envelope's flap and reached for the contents. He looked down at an old photo of his mother and a man. He quickly turned it over. Mr. and Mrs. Elam Troyer.

So, this is my father. He stared down at the photo and his heart filled with emotion…sadness. His parents' tale had been tragic indeed. He examined the picture, hoping to identify traits in himself. Rosemary was correct, he did somewhat favor his father. He had his eyes, just as his mother had written. But Sally hadn't seemed to notice. Had Elam changed that much over the years?

He reached for the one thing remaining in the envelope. A note in his mother's handwriting was attached to the outside of the smaller envelope.

William, this is a letter your father sent to me years after Peter and I were happily married. I never opened it, so I do not know what it says. I don't need to. Somehow, I feel the words are meant for you. Love, your mother

In a way, he dreaded opening the letter. What if the words contained therein were words he'd rather not hear?

"Well, what does it say?" Uncle George entered the library with two steaming mugs. He handed one to Will.

In exchange, Will handed him the letter.

His uncle's eyes roamed the note his mother had written then he turned the envelope over. "It's not open." Uncle George frowned.

Will sighed. "I know."

His uncle handed the envelope back and Will gave him the picture. "Yep. That's your father, all right." He nodded, then shook his head. He handed the photo back.

Will stared at his uncle. "I'm thinking of not opening it," he admitted.

"Why not?"

He shrugged. "I don't know. If Mom didn't open it...I mean, it was written to *her*."

"True. But she kept it for *you*."

"You're right." He took a breath and slid his finger under the flap.

He silently read the words penned to his mother many years ago.

Will sat mesmerized for several minutes, staring at the letter in his hands. He shook his head. "I can't believe this."

"What? What does it say?"

Will handed the letter to his uncle and watched his reaction as he read the words.

His uncle's gaze pierced his. "Oh, wow, William. I had no idea."

TWENTY-SIX

*W*ill hadn't originally planned on picking up Sally at the train station, but Uncle George had said he wouldn't be able to do it today. Fortunately, the Lancaster station wasn't too far from the house, and they wouldn't have to be in the car alone together for too long. Seeing Sally again would be bittersweet, to say the least.

He glanced at his watch and rose from the bench. Sally's train would be arriving any minute if it was on schedule. He began pacing the lobby, trying to determine what exactly he would say to her.

A loud horn drew his attention to the tracks. Sally's train had arrived.

Saloma looked out the window as the train rolled into the station. Will had written in his letter that his uncle would be picking her up, but she didn't see him anywhere. She hoped she wouldn't be left stranded.

"Well, looks like this is our stop," Pam said. Saloma had enjoyed a pleasant conversation with the woman, who was traveling with her two children. "I don't know about you, but we're ready to get out and walk a bit."

Sally smiled in response.

"It was nice to meet you, Saloma. I hope you have a nice Thanksgiving with your family."

"*Denki.* You, too."

As the train car came to a complete stop, Sally clutched her travel bag to her chest. Slowly, she followed Pam and the other passengers to the unloading zone. She looked around the platform, but didn't see Will's uncle anywhere.

"Hey, beautiful," a voice from behind her called.

She quickly spun around. "Will?"

Will's handsome smile greeted her.

Maybe this was a bad idea. Seeing Will just made her fall in love with him all over again. "Hello, brother," she said, mostly to remind herself.

Will frowned, then reached for her bag. "Here. Let me carry that."

"Where are you parked?"

He tilted his head toward the station's entrance. "This way."

They remained silent as they walked to his Jeep. He opened the door for her and a wash of memories came back. Yes, being with Will was a bad idea. Why had he picked her up instead of his uncle?

"Your uncle couldn't come?" she vocalized her thoughts.

"Don't want to ride with me, huh?" His words sounded like he was teasing her, but his tone did not. "He had to work," he said flatly.

What was wrong with him?

"*Denki* for picking me up."

He nodded without a verbal reply.

They rode in silence for what seemed like an eternity.

Finally, she couldn't take it anymore. "What's wrong, Will?"

He stared at her. "You're asking me what's wrong? I think you know."

Did he mean what she thought he meant or was there another issue?

She swallowed. "Are you upset with me?"

"How was Kentucky?" He raised a brow.

"Was that a yes or a no?"

Will remained silent. He was clearly avoiding her question.

He is *mad at me!*

She stared at him. "I don't understand."

"Yeah, well, that makes two of us."

He pulled up to the farm and came to an abrupt stop.

She opened the Jeep's door. "Why did you ask me to come home if you don't want me here?"

"I didn't say that."

"You didn't have to." She slammed the door. "Kentucky was great, by the way. In fact, I wish I was there right now." Saloma stormed to the house and hurried to her room.

As soon as she heard Will's Jeep peel out of the driveway, she broke down in tears.

"Well?"

Will met Uncle George's gaze across the table. "Well, what?"

"Did you talk to her?"

"Is that why you wanted me to pick her up? So we could talk?"

"That was part of it."

"Yes and no. We didn't get anywhere, if that's what you mean."

"You *did* invite her to come home for Thanksgiving, remember?"

"I know. I know. I guess I just envisioned things differently."

"We *can* cancel, but that would be rude."

"No, I don't want to cancel. I just need to figure what on earth I'm going to say to her."

"How about the truth?"

He patted his uncle on the back. "Now *that* is a novel idea, Uncle George."

TWENTY-SEVEN

W paced the floor. Sally and her family would be arriving any minute with Uncle George.

He surveyed the perfectly set table. His mother's china set was rarely in use, and he was pleased to have it for this special occasion.

"Marita, are you sure you don't need help with anything?"

"You just asked that five minutes ago, Mr. Griffith. And, no, I don't require your assistance." She studied him briefly. "Why don't you take a walk out in the garden to try to relieve some of that anxiety?"

"Great idea."

Will quickly exited the house and walked out into his uncle's stunning backyard. Leaves of red, yellow, and brown now covered the landscape that had just been cleared yesterday. A slight breeze blew. He noted the crisp fall air and the changing of seasons.

Will inhaled deeply and offered thanksgiving to his Creator for his many blessings, several of whom would be arriving in just a short time. *God, my life is in Your hands.*

Another gust caused more leaves to tremble and cascade to the ground. Out of his peripheral vision, he caught sight of the swaying swing. The swing where he and Sally had shared their first kiss.

"William, your guests have arrived," Marita's voice called from the sunroom door.

Will nodded and followed after Marita. "Coming."

The brief walk had somewhat quelled his nervousness, but his anxiousness over seeing Sally had not dispelled.

Will greeted each of his family members upon his entrance. All received a proper greeting, except for Sally, who he simply nodded to. He'd have a private discussion with her later.

His uncle announced, "I'd love to give you all a tour of my home, but Marita has informed me that dinner is ready, so the tour will have to wait. Everyone, please take your seats."

Will noticed the place cards Marita had set out, a lovely addition to the already-elegant table.

"Rosemary," Uncle George pulled out the chair for Will's stepmother.

Will followed suit and pulled out a chair for one of his sisters, and they continued to do so until all their guests were seated.

His uncle nodded and reached for the hands of those beside him. "I'd like to say the blessing," Uncle George informed them, "but, before I do, I'd like to offer you all an apology. Especially you, Saloma."

Sally briefly glanced at Will then nodded to his uncle.

Uncle George continued, "I've judged you all and your people unfairly. When Elam left, we had a falling out of sorts, and it tainted my view of all the Amish people. I believe that Bishop Mast was wrong in advising him to leave my sister. Nevertheless, I believe that God works out things for the best, even when we get in the way of His plan for our lives.

"You all have been nothing but gracious to William and me, and we appreciate the wonderful hospitality you have so unselfishly lavished upon us. So, please, accept my most humble apologies."

Each member of the Troyer family smiled and nodded their acceptance.

"Let us give thanks now," Uncle George said.

Will's pleased smile reached his uncle, and they all bowed their heads.

"Please join hands," Uncle George requested.

Will held his hands out to those at his side, Sally and Clara. Clara happily took her half-brother's hand, but Sally stared at Will hesitantly. He nodded, giving permission, and she reluctantly placed her hand in his. He gently closed his fingers around hers.

Saloma pried her eyes open just a little, as Will's uncle said the blessing. Will's eyes were closed, so she took the opportunity to stare at her hand in Will's. His behavior lately had been strange, to say the least. But, now, as she held his hand, it felt like the world was right again – at least, between the two of them.

As everyone opened their eyes and the food was passed around, Sally kept replaying the scene at the train station. Or on their way home from the station, more accurately. For the life of her, she couldn't figure out why Will was upset with her.

Elam. Yes, that had to be it. One of her sisters must've mentioned she'd been seeing Elam. But why would that matter to her brother? Maybe he was hoping it would take her longer to get over him. If he only knew her heart on the matter. Perhaps they could have a heart-to-heart conversation later and discuss their feelings and expectations. Whatever the matter was, they needed to get it out in the open so they could put this all behind them and move on with their lives.

Sally's mother and sisters insisted on helping Marita with the putting away of the meal and dish washing. Will took this opportunity to speak to his uncle about the remainder of the afternoon. Uncle George agreed to give Will's Amish family a tour of the house and the grounds, while Will and Sally went for a walk.

"Sally," Will called her from the kitchen's entrance. "Come."

Saloma did as bidden, and she and Will stepped out into the backyard.

He reached for her hand but she shook her head. "No, Will."

He began walking down one of the treed paths with Sally at his side. The leaves crunched beneath their feet, but he paid them no mind. "Fine. Have it your way."

She stopped and turned to him. "Will, what's going on with you? Why have you been acting so strange lately? Why are you behaving like you're still in love with me?"

"Maybe *I am* still in love with you, Sally. Maybe I'm not about to lose you to someone else."

"No! Don't do this." Tears pricked her eyes. "We can't be together, Will. You *know* that."

Will's jaw clenched. She was a better actress than he'd thought.

He raised a brow. "Do I really? Or is there something *you know* that you aren't telling me?"

"What are you talking about, Will?"

"The one little secret you conveniently 'forgot' to tell me about? You know, if you didn't want to be with me in the first place, you could have just said so." He frowned. "It would have been much easier if you would have just come out with the truth instead of living a lie. Here you had me believing that a relationship between us is impossible. But maybe it is, huh? Maybe it's impossible because *you* want it to be."

"What do you mean? What secret?"

Will stepped close and caressed her face.

"Will, I honestly have no idea what you're talking about. And I wish you would stop this! It's not right and it's not fair." She pushed his hand away.

"I know the truth, Sally."

"What truth?"

"That you're adopted."

Saloma gasped and stepped backward. "That's absolutely ridiculous! Why would you make up something so...so...preposterous? Are you really *that* desperate, Will?" She scowled.

He reached into his pocket and pulled out his father's letter. "No, Sally. I'm not the desperate one in this equation. You can't pretend anymore. It's all right here."

She stared at Will as though searching for answers in the depths of his soul. "What is this?"

Will watched as she took the letter from his hand and read it aloud.

"Sandra,

Greetings in the name of the Lord.

Thought I'd write you a letter after I saw you at the store the other day. I saw you before you turned my way and you seemed to be content. That is, until you saw me and my fraa.

I want you to know that I'm not happy about what I'd done to you. My heart hurts too. I 'spect it's something neither of us will get over too soon. Tell your brother George that I'm sorry too. I know I messed up a lot of things when I left my Amish roots and jumped the fence.

Thank you for not saying anything at the store. My fraa, Rosemary, she don't know about us. I haven't had a heart to tell her. Our *boppli* that you saw, that was little Saloma. A special blessing she was to us. I was for sure and certain God had been angry with me after I left you. Rosemary and me couldn't have no *kinner*, or that's what we thought. So we adopted little Saloma.

I hope you'll forgive me for what I done to you. I know I did you wrong in a big way and God weren't pleased.

I hope you're happy with your new life. I see you got you a boy, so I'm guessing you're hitched again. That's good. That's real good. He seemed like a fine boy. It got me wondering what a boy of our making would have looked like. But I shouldn't be thinking on those things. It ain't right.

Anyway, that's all I got to say, I reckon.

Goodbye, Sandra.

Elam"

Sally's mouth hung open. "This letter was from my father?"

Will nodded. "To my mother."

She stared at Will. "He…he said I was adopted. I don't believe it." She shook her head.

"What? Are you saying you didn't know?" Will couldn't help the skepticism in his voice. "You're nearly twenty and you didn't know you were adopted?"

Tears surfaced in her eyes. "No! I didn't know. This is the first I've heard anything about it."

His arms crossed his chest. "Why would your parents not have told you?"

"I don't know. I don't understand this." She brushed away a tear.

He frowned.

She looked into Will's eyes, a disappointed expression on her face. "So, you thought that *I knew* all this and I was keeping it from you? How and why do you think I would do that, Will? When we had to break up, it hurt me just as much as it hurt you, if not more."

"Yeah. That's why you ran to that Amish guy, right? You began courting before I could even breathe again, Sally!"

"Do you mean Elam? I was trying to get over you. I was trying to get *my brother* out of my head. *You* even told me to start courting again! Besides, Elam and I are just friends."

"He hasn't kissed you?" His gaze pierced hers.

Sally's cheeks darkened. "That's not fair, Will. You said–"

"*You* said you were *just* friends."

"Yes, we've kissed."

He shoved his hands into his pockets. "So, now what? Where does that leave us?"

She shrugged. "Well…maybe we should have never been seeing each other in the first place. You are *Englisch*, after all."

"So, that's it? We're done?" Will couldn't help the moisture that began to gather in his eyes. He swallowed hard.

Will wanted to protest. In his pocket, his finger brushed the ring he'd purchased for Sally before she'd gone to Kentucky. How many times had he dreamed of giving it to her since he'd found out the truth? But now she was no longer interested?

Saloma stared off into the distance. "I don't know. I need to think about it, Will."

He pulled the ring from his pocket and placed it into her hand. "You do that." He leaned over and kissed her cheek and quickly disappeared into his uncle's house. He'd hoped to some-day build a home together with Sally, but it seemed the only thing they'd managed to build together was a house of cards.

TWENTY-EIGHT

*W*ill felt a rocking sensation, like he was out on a fishing boat in the deep sea.

"William, get up. You're going to be late for church," Uncle George urged.

Will rolled over and grasped his comforter. "I'm not going."

His uncle frowned. "I'd hoped to go with you today."

Will raised his head. "You did?"

Uncle George nodded.

"Okay," he groaned. "I'll go."

"What's wrong, William?"

Will threw his blankets off. "I'd rather not talk about it now."

"Are you upset that Saloma returned to Kentucky?"

Will lifted his hand, indicating the discussion was over.

"I understand." Uncle George walked to the door. "Listen, William. If you need me, I'm here to talk. Anytime."

"I appreciate that." Will walked to his closet and pulled out a pair of khakis and a long-sleeved button-down.

If Uncle George was *finally* going to attend church with him, Will decided even the deepest depression wouldn't keep him away. He'd been praying for his uncle for years now, and to finally see his prayer answered gave Will a much-needed spark of hope.

Perhaps he and Sally could somehow make it work between them. The fact that it hadn't worked out between his parents worried Will even further. Was he kidding himself thinking that he and Sally could make it? After all, they had even more obstacles than his parents had.

He hadn't heard from Sally since she'd gone back to Kentucky two weeks ago. The silence was driving him mad. Had he been a fool to hope for the impossible? Perhaps their romantic relationship wasn't part of God's will. When he'd found out that Sally had been adopted, he'd thought that was a sure sign that God was in this. Had he been wrong?

Saloma's back began aching as she waited for Minister Swartz to finish his sermon. She bowed her head and fingered Will's ring in her pocket. Oh, how she missed him. Even with all his craziness. A life with Will sounded so good, but it also frightened her.

She wasn't accustomed to the *Englisch* ways. What if she became homesick, like her father had, and wanted to return home? She could never see herself divorcing for *any* reason, but what if her father had thought the same way? Was an honest love enough to stand the trials life would bring?

There was one thing, though, that gave her an advantage over her father. She hadn't been baptized yet. If she left the church now, her family wouldn't be required to shun her outright. If there ever was a decision to make, it was now.

Dear Gott, *please guide me. Please show me what your will is for my life.*

Saloma raised her head and discovered the service was almost over. Elam's gaze caught hers and she lifted a brief smile. If only he knew the turmoil churning in her soul. She was certain sure poor Elam's kind heart would not escape unscathed.

"William," Pastor Rob's cheerful voice greeted him. "It was so good to see your uncle here."

Will looked to his uncle, who stood chatting with a couple of other men in the church. "Yes. It was an answer to prayer." He hesitated. "Pastor, do you have a couple of minutes?"

"Certainly. Let's go sit in the front pew."

Will nodded and followed Pastor Rob to the front of the church auditorium.

"What's on your mind? I haven't seen you around in a while."

Will covered his face then looked up at the pastor. "I've been going through quite a bit lately, and, honestly, I've been depressed. My life's been kind of crazy."

Pastor Rob nodded. "I can relate to that."

"It mostly has to do with Sally."

"Ah, I remember. The Amish girl who worked for us for a couple of weeks."

"She's the one."

"Your girlfriend, right?"

"Ex." Will frowned.

"Oh."

"That's kind of the reason I wanted to talk to you. Are there any rules in the Bible about who you marry, besides being equally yoked?" Will rubbed the back of his neck. "I mean, like about marrying relatives and such."

"Relatives?"

Will grimaced. "Well, I learned that Sally is my sister. Sort of. She's my adopted half-sister."

"Adopted half-sister?" Pastor Rob stared at the wall, as though trying to figure out the relation in his head.

"It's a long story. Basically, my mother and biological father had me, divorced, he remarried an Amish woman, and they adopted Sally."

"So she isn't blood-related in *any* way?"

"Not that I know of." Will shrugged. "I mean, aren't we all related in one way or another if you go back far enough?"

"Basically. We all came from Adam and Eve." Pastor Rob sighed then leveled his gaze at Will. "I've got to tell you, William, things like this are typically taboo as far as society is concerned. Have you discussed the possible legal implications with your uncle?"

Will swallowed. "Legal implications? I didn't even think about that. Do you think the two of us marrying might be illegal?" The thought sounded ludicrous. He hadn't even known Sally existed a year ago.

"I don't know. However, I do know that marrying siblings and first cousins is against the law."

"But I thought that was because of possible medical and genetic problems. If Sally and I aren't blood-related, I don't see how there could be a problem."

"I honestly can't advise you regarding this, William. I'm not an expert in the law."

"Okay. I'll have to talk to my uncle about it then. I'm guessing that he must not have seen an issue with it, because he hasn't said anything." Will glanced around in search of his uncle. "Well, thank you for your time, Pastor."

"I'm sorry I couldn't advise you further."

"I understand. Between you and me, how do *you* feel about this? Would you be willing to marry Sally and me?"

"If there's no law against it, I don't have a problem with it."

Will smiled and shook Pastor Rob's hand. "Thanks, Pastor."

TWENTY-NINE

Elam approached Saloma before the singing began and asked if he could take her home this evening. They hadn't been on a buggy ride since she'd returned from Pennsylvania, and a bit of nervousness fluttered in her stomach.

"*Jah*, Elam. I will ride with you," she'd said.

They'd only had one conversation since Thanksgiving and she'd told him all about finding out about her adoption. Elam's enthusiasm seemed to dampen when she'd revealed this detail. Had he thought about the possibility of she and Will getting back together?

Now that the singing was over and they sat side by side, Saloma's thoughts drifted to her time with Will. She'd been so upset with him, she didn't even bid him a proper goodbye.

"Other than finding out about your adoption, how did your visit home go? You didn't really tell me about that. Did you see Will?"

"I'd rather not discuss it." She huffed.

"I think you should. I can tell you want to," Elam coaxed, lifting an eyebrow.

"Well, first of all, Will was acting like some lovesick puppy."

"I would too." He grinned.

"Yeah, well, when you're *related* to someone, there are limits."

"I agree." Elam nodded.

"Well, then he accuses me of lying to him about being adopted! I hadn't even known I was adopted. He knew before I did." She threw her hands in the air.

"Did you talk to your mother about that?"

"Of course. She said she and *Dat* never said anything to me about it because they didn't feel it was necessary."

"Do you think they should have told you? Would you have wanted to know?"

"I don't know. I grew up in a good home. What more could I ask for?"

"Nothin', I guess. But wouldn't you like to meet your birth mother?"

"Maybe." She shrugged.

"So...what are you planning to do?"

Sally reached into her pocket and grasped the ring Will had given her. "I don't know. I'm still angry with Will right now."

"Saloma, you're in love with him. If not, you wouldn't be this upset."

She shook her head. "It can never work out between us."

"I don't believe that any more than you do, Saloma."

"I'm happy courting you." Did her voice sound as unconvincing to Elam as it did to her own ears?

"Are you really?" Elam's honest eyes pierced hers. "Saloma, you said we were free to court, but you've never been free to love. Your heart is locked in a cage and only one person holds the key. And it's not me. I'd hoped and prayed that things could work out between the two of us, but it's plain to see that you're still in love with him. And he's crazy for you. Literally." Elam laughed, then held Saloma's gaze. "Now that there's no good reason for the two of you not to be together, I need to let you go. If I let you go, you will be free to love. I'd be a fool to step in and hinder the plans God has for you. Go to Will, Saloma. You have my blessing."

Saloma broke down in tears. Elam had been nothing but good and kind and understanding. It pained her to break his heart.

"Don't worry about me. I have other options," he winked, but she heard the disappointment in his tone.

"*Denki*, Elam. Thank you for understanding."

"Hey, what are friends for?"

"Elam, if Will and I weren't–"

"Don't say it, Saloma. Just go, okay." He gently wiped her tears with the pads of his thumbs. "I'll be fine. I promise."

She nodded and scurried out of Elam's buggy.

Uncle George took a sip of his water. "William, I'd like to thank you for inviting me to church. I can't tell you how good it felt. I haven't been this energized in years."

Will smiled at his uncle. "I'm so glad. Does this mean you'll be attending with me more often?"

"Definitely. I feel like a fire has been kindled in my soul." He dabbed his chin with the cloth napkin.

Will had never seen his uncle so content. It thrilled his heart more than words could say. "That's wonderful."

"I saw you talking with the pastor this morning."

Will sighed. "Uncle George, do you think there are any laws forbidding Sally and me to marry?"

His uncle set his fork down. "Are you and Saloma *that* serious? I thought she'd gone back to Kentucky."

"You're right, she did. I was just thinking, *if* there was a chance for us."

"I hadn't thought about it. Honestly, I'd hoped you'd find someone else, William. With all that your mother went through, I'd hate to see you have a similar experience."

"Just because that happened with my parents doesn't mean it will happen with us."

"That's true. But there's so much risk involved. William, if you could just find someone else…"

"Uncle George, I love Sally. And I'm quite certain she loves me too. Now that I know we're not blood-related, I'm hoping beyond hope there's a chance for us."

His uncle rubbed his forehead. "Are you *really* sure you want to pursue this, William?"

"I'm absolutely positive. I can't stand the thought of living without Sally. Have you ever loved anyone that much, Uncle George?"

"I can't say I have."

"Will you please consider looking into this for me?"

"If that's what you'd like, William."

"Thank you, Uncle."

Saloma agreed to stay on at the school until they could find a replacement for her. They'd implied it would be good if she could at least stay until Christmas break. The leaders and parents expressed their disappointment at seeing her go. She would surely miss her students and the wonderful people here in her aunt's Kentucky Amish community, but she knew she'd miss kind Elam more than anyone, for sure and certain.

Elam had already begun courting another girl, according to her cousin Rebecca. Saloma decided not to attend any more of the singings while she was here. If she was to eventually become *Englisch*, she'd have to learn to do without all the customs she'd grown up with.

But she was certain that loving Will, and receiving his love in return, would be worth it all.

Will stared at the papers on Uncle George's desk. *This can't be right.*

"I really am sorry, William."

He knew his uncle had spoken, but he couldn't understand the words.

The only words he could hear were the ones inside his head. *No, this can't be true. Sally and I can't marry?* This was not acceptable. Not acceptable at all.

"What...I don't see..." he couldn't even put together a protest.

"You marrying Saloma would be illegal," Uncle George spelled it out.

"No."

"I'm sorry."

"I can't accept this."

Uncle George placed a hand on Will's shoulder. "We have to, William. It's the law."

"It's none of their business who I marry!"

His uncle sighed. "Even so..."

"We don't have to tell them, right? We could just marry and not say anything." Will didn't care if he sounded desperate. He had a chance to be with Sally and, now, the one chance, that one thread of hope, was being snatched right from his hand. "Who would tell? How would they know?"

"You'd be breaking the law, William. You could go to prison."

Prison? Why, God?

He shot up from the table. "This is stupid! We didn't even grow up in the same household. I could see if we were related by blood, but we're not. We're virtually strangers. We didn't even know each other existed, for Pete's sake! How can they do this? I don't understand how they think it's their right to define who I choose to marry."

"I don't know what to tell you, William. I cannot change the laws."

Will paced the floor. There had to be another way. There *had* to be. "Could we marry somewhere else? Is this illegal everywhere?"

"I don't know. I can look into it for you."

"Please, Uncle George?"

"Sure. If that's what you'd like. I'll help you any way I can, son."

THIRTY

$\mathcal{P}$aloma smiled to herself as she glanced over the seat at her driver. Wouldn't Will be surprised! She still hadn't contacted him at all. The last time they'd seen each other was on Thanksgiving Day, almost a month ago. Now, it was just a few days before Christmas, and Sally thought this would be a good time to surprise her beloved.

"It's right up here," she informed the driver. She couldn't help the enthusiasm in her voice.

It would be wonderful to see Will again and bring a smile to his handsome face. The last time she'd seen him, he seemed so downtrodden. Now, she imagined him taking her into his arms and kissing her full on the mouth, the way they had before she'd first gone to Kentucky. She glanced down at Will's promise ring on her finger, and her smile brightened. This would be a brand new start for the both of them, and she couldn't wait.

The driver pulled into the driveway of Will's uncle's home. Saloma handed him the monies due and clutched her bag.

She took a calming breath and walked to the home's entrance. The scent of pine emanated from the wreath on the door, reminding her that Christmas was just around the corner. Her family had never used wreaths; they'd always decorated simply with just a small table for gifts and maybe a pine bough or two.

A chilly breeze blew when Will's housekeeper opened the door. "You are Sally." Marita smiled.

"Yes. I'm here to see Will." Saloma tried to tamper her grin, but failed miserably.

"He is in his room. Come." They stepped into the cozy home and Sally noticed the large, brightly-decorated Christmas tree. Soft music played and a euphoric warmth filled her being. Marita led the way through the foyer, past the family room, and down the hallway. She smiled and nodded, leaving Saloma standing at the door alone.

Saloma hesitantly knocked. Maybe surprising him wasn't such a good idea. What if he wasn't dressed properly? What if he was in the shower? What if–

"Sally?" Will frowned. "What are you doing here?"

Saloma's excitement immediately dwindled. "You...you are not happy to see me?" She glanced down at the ring on her finger and felt like a fool.

Will's eyes went to her finger as well. He lifted a brief half smile. "You're wearing my ring," he said flatly.

"Yes, I...I wanted to surprise you. I am home now."

"Sally, I don't know what to say." He stepped out of his room. "Let's go talk in the library, okay?"

Why was Will acting so strangely? Why hadn't he engulfed her in a hug? Why hadn't he kissed her lips? He didn't even seem pleased to see her.

The confidence she previously had melted away like a crayon in the afternoon sun, leaving only a dark spot as evidence to where it had once been. Instead of the warmth of the sun, she now only felt a chill.

"I thought you'd be glad to see me." Tears pricked her eyes.

William sighed. "I'm sorry, Sally, but you and I can't be together. It's not possible."

"What do you mean?" One of the tears escaped her eyelashes and trailed her cheek, its saltiness meeting the corner of her mouth.

"In order for us to marry, we would have to break the law."

Could Will's words be true? "I don't understand. How?"

"We're siblings, according to the law. Siblings can't marry – under *any* circumstance."

"But we are not *really* brother and sister." She frowned.

Will's hands clenched his hair, as though he wanted to pull it out. "I know that and you know that. But it doesn't matter to the government, Sally."

"That's not right."

"I know it's not right, but there's nothing we can do." He grimaced and turned away. "You would have been better off staying in Kentucky."

Saloma's body shook with a sob. What was she going to do now?

Will wished with all his might that he could take Sally into his arms and hold her close until the daylight faded into night. If only he could kiss her tears away. When she arrived, she'd seemed so excited. He hated being the one to snatch away her joy.

He glanced down at her hand. She was wearing his ring! Did this mean she'd decided to become his? Was she ready to take the next step and accept his proposal?

He'd marry her today if he could. If only he could…

Why, God? I don't understand.

He looked at Sally, who stood crying. His voice was gentle. "I'm sorry, Sally. I've been praying…hoping for a miracle." He shook his head. "I don't know what God is doing. I'm really having a difficult time with this. I'm trying to trust Him."

She sucked in a breath and swiped at a tear. "Do you think *He* doesn't want us to be married?"

"Maybe there's something really bad in our future. Maybe we'll end up like my parents."

Her chin quivered. "I wouldn't *ever* leave you, Will."

He reached over and caressed her cheek. "I feel the same way. To me, marriage isn't something you can get out of. It's not even an option. It's for better or worse. It's for a lifetime. I guess my parents didn't see it that way.

"The way I see it, it would not only be a covenant between us, but with God as well. The Bible says that a strand of three cords is not easily broken. I think that's what's missing in a lot of marriages – the God strand. It's nearly impossible when you try to do it without God."

Oh, how he wanted to hold her. Just to feel her in his arms... *Stop it!* he chided himself.

"I wish there was a way. I did ask my uncle to see if perhaps we could marry in another state. We might have to move..."

Her eyes widened. "Move?"

"Would you be willing to? I mean, if it's the only way? We could visit Pennsylvania as often as we wanted to."

"Do you think it's possible?" He heard the hope in Sally's voice.

"Oh, I hope so. Will you pray with me, Sally? Will you pray that God will make a way for us?"

"*Jah.* I will pray for certain."

"Good." He smiled gently. "Let's not lose hope, okay?"

"No. Never."

Will's Jeep rolled to a stop in front of the Troyer residence.

"I'll pick you up on Christmas Eve." Will had already been pondering what gift he'd like to give Sally.

"Okay." Sally lifted a half smile.

"Your mom will be okay with it, right?"

"You will have me home early, *jah*?"

"As early as you need to be home."

"I'm not sure yet. We will leave in the morning?"

His gaze met hers. "I'd like to spend all day with you, if possible."

Sally blushed. "Is that a *gut* idea?"

"I think it's a great idea. Being with you will be the best Christmas present I'll receive this year. Can you be ready by eight?"

"Eight?" Her eyes bulged.

"I'd like to take you to breakfast at Shady Maple. Have you been there before?"

Sally's head shook.

"You're in for a wonderful treat." He smiled.

Will opened the door for Sally. He longed to embrace her but he wouldn't. "Goodbye."

THIRTY-ONE

"Did you share your news with Saloma?" Uncle George's brow shot up.

"Oh, no, I forgot!" Will chuckled. "I guess I was just so surprised to see her that I didn't even think about it. But I can tell her in a couple of days, because I invited her to spend Christmas Eve day with me."

"Do you think that's wise, William?"

At times, Uncle George's patronizing voice rattled Will's nerves. "At this point, I don't care. I want to spend the holidays with Sally, and I intend to do just that." Will realized his flippant attitude and toned down a bit. "Don't worry, we're not going to do anything we shouldn't."

"That's only part of the issue. The more of your heart you give to Sally, the less chance you have of escaping unscathed."

"I'm willing to take that risk."

Uncle George's gaze met his. "Truthfully, I'm worried about you, William. You've been so depressed lately. If things don't work out between you and Saloma–"

"Then I will trust that it's not God's will. Until we've exhausted all our resources and God gives a definite 'no', Sally and I are hoping and praying for a miracle. God can work out impossible situations. I'm counting on a miracle. I know God will work this out."

Uncle George sighed and shook his head. "For your sake, I hope you're right."

Will pulled into the parking lot of Shady Maple Smorgasbord and stole a glance at Sally. He sighed. *Thy will be done, Lord.* He constantly reminded himself of this very thing. He was trusting God's will, or at least trying to. *For we walk by faith, not by sight.*

"*Ach*, there's a buggy here. I wonder if I know who it is." Sally brightened.

That was the one thing that worried Will most about their possible union. The Amish were big on community and fellowship. If they ended up marrying, and Sally left her Amish district, their dealings with the Amish would be minimal. And, although most would not be required to shun Sally outright, she said that some of the more strict Amish still would. Will hoped that he would be enough for her.

He opened the door to the restaurant and escorted Sally inside. "Would you like to browse the gift shop?"

"Let's look after we eat, *jah*?"

"Whatever you'd like." Will smiled. He couldn't describe it, but being in Sally's presence made him feel complete somehow. He briefly wondered if this was how Adam felt after God created a helpmeet for him. He'd had God and the whole world before Eve, but after God brought his wife to him, Creation was complete. God knew exactly what he needed and provided for him.

"Will?"

He turned at the vaguely familiar voice. "Minister Fisher?"

The man smiled. "Jonathan."

"I remember." Will turned to Sally. "Jonathan, this is Saloma Troyer."

"*Gut* to meet you." He turned to his *fraa*. "This is my Susie."

Will and Saloma both greeted Jonathan's wife.

Jonathan eyed Will. "Did you ever receive an answer to your impossible question?"

"I'm still praying about it."

"I've been thinking on that some too. I'm glad we ran into each other. Why don't you and Saloma join us at our table, and we can talk about this further?"

Will turned to Sally. "Do you mind?"

"*Nee.*"

They requested a table for four instead of two, like Will had originally planned. But maybe it was better if he and Sally didn't spend too much time alone together.

Jonathan took a sip of his coffee and eyed Will from across the table. "Did you mention to me before that you were adopted?"

Will stared toward the ceiling. "I don't recall. But yes, Sally and I are both adopted." Will's eyes widened and a new thought dawned on him. "Wait a minute. If I was adopted by Peter, it would mean that I'm no longer Elam's son, correct?"

Jonathan shrugged. "I don't know. I guess so."

"If I'm no longer Elam's son, then Sally and I aren't brother and sister." Will stared at Sally and his grin broadened. "Will you excuse me for a moment? I have to make a phone call."

Jonathan smiled. "Sure."

Will hurried out to the parking lot, typing in Uncle George's cell number as rapidly as possible.

His uncle answered on the third ring. "Hello?"

"Uncle George, I'm legally adopted by Peter, right?"

"Of course."

"Well, then, doesn't that mean that Saloma and I can't be siblings?"

There was a pause on the other end.

"Uncle George?" Will paced the parking lot, ignoring the sudden gust of cold air.

"I'm thinking," he said. "I'm not an expert in family law, but I can call my colleague. He'd know. It'll probably have to wait until after the holidays."

At this moment in time, Will felt like he might burst if he had to wait that long. But he would if he had to. "Do you have my adoption documents at the house?"

"I believe so."

"Will you get those out so I can look at them when Sally and I return from breakfast, please?"

"Sure, William."

"Great. Thanks, Uncle George!"

He clicked off the phone, and began humming a song that had been on his heart since the last church service. It just so happened that last Sunday's music special at church was about God making a way when there seemed to be no way. It was almost as though God chose the song just for him and his circumstances. Had He prompted the singer to choose that song just to encourage Will's heart? It sure seemed so. God was so good!

He rushed inside to finish his meal with his guests, but his heart soared, and he couldn't erase the grin from his face for the rest of the morning. God was definitely working on his behalf!

THIRTY-TWO

"Thank you for the dinner, Marita. It was wonderful," Uncle George called out as his housekeeper left for the evening. "I hope you have a magnificent Christmas with your family."

"I worry about you and Mr. Griffith, sir. Will you be okay?"

"William and I survived longer than a week without you last year, so we'll be all right. Besides, it wouldn't hurt us to miss a meal or two," Will's uncle teased. "We'll manage, just don't be any longer than you need to."

"Very well, sir. Have a happy holiday."

"Goodbye, Marita." Uncle George watched as Marita left, then turned to Will and Sally. "Now, the three of us have some matters to discuss."

Will nodded confidently.

"Let's gather around the hearth in the great room; the fire is burning nicely. I'll get the documents."

Will's eyes followed as Uncle George moved toward his office. He turned to Sally and took a prayerful breath. "Come."

He held out his hand, and he and Sally walked to the great room. Will loved the large, comfortable couches that surrounded the hearth. He had many favorite places in the house, and after the library, this came in a close second.

Will pulled Sally down next to him. "Well, what do you think?"

"I think we can trust God." She smiled.

"You're right. Whatever happens will be God's will, right?" Will sounded as though he were trying to convince himself.

Uncle George walked into the room and sat on the sofa adjacent to William and Saloma. He eyed his nephew. "Did you share your news with Sally?"

Will shook his head, then turned to Sally. "I finished school." His uncle's countenance evidenced obvious pride.

"That's *wunderbaar*, Will."

"Yes, William did very well." His uncle beamed.

"Okay, now I'd like to give you my Christmas gift." Uncle George reached across the oversized coffee table and handed Will an envelope – the kind that would hold a greeting card.

Will's puzzled expression caused his uncle to chuckle. "Go ahead. Open it."

Will examine the plain red envelope, slid his finger under the envelope's flap, and removed a Christmas card. An elegant Thomas Kincaid print of an old-town snow-covered Christmas scene graced the front.

He read the words aloud, "To William and Saloma, Merry Christmas! May the two of you have a wonderful life. Together.

Sincerely, Uncle George." Will reread the message, attempting to decipher its meaning.

"Uh, thank you." Will glanced at Sally, and she nodded in agreement.

Uncle George then pulled out an official-looking document from the large manila envelope at his side. He handed it to William.

Will scanned the document until he came to the signature at the bottom. "Elam Troyer?"

"That, William, is your golden ticket."

"What do you mean?"

"Well, apparently, your birth father *knew* you existed. He would have had to sign over his parental rights in order for Peter to adopt you."

"So, what does this mean?" Sally piped up, an uncertain expression on her face.

"That means that Elam Troyer's property belongs to your mother." Uncle George smiled. "As well as a couple other things."

"But what about what was written on those papers my mother received? They had Will's name on them." Sally frowned.

A thrill danced up Will's arms and traveled straight through to his soul. What implications did this new revelation have?

George grimaced. "The papers were filed in error. Apparently, the presiding attorney found William's original birth certificate, stating that Sandra and Elam Troyer were his parents. He didn't realized that Elam had terminated his parental rights, thus relinquishing all interest in the child. By that document, any and all ties are broken.

"When Peter adopted William, he received a brand new birth certificate. By law, Peter is William's father. By law, William has a new lineage. His old lineage no longer exists."

Will's grin broadened even more. "So, not only am I *not* Elam's son, I also have no rights to his property."

"Yes, that is what this means," his uncle agreed.

Will perked up. "I'm perfectly happy with that! I didn't want the property in the first place." He turned to Sally. "It looks like we are all receiving great gifts this Christmas!"

Will looked his uncle in the eye, his gaze completely sober. He enunciated each word, as though he were stirring molasses in the wintry cold. "If I am Peter's son, then Sally and I are not brother and sister, by law. Am I correct?"

Uncle George smiled. "Absolutely."

"Hallelujah!" Will jumped up from the couch. "Wow! I couldn't have asked for a better solution. Thank you, Uncle George."

"I'll be sending you my fee next week," he teased.

"I'd gladly pay it!"

"Seriously, though, I'm not the one you two should be thanking."

Will and Sally nodded. "Oh, yes, you better believe I will be thanking God many times this night and for the rest of our lives!" Will turned to Sally. "Isn't God good, Sally?"

Sally's eyes filled with tears. "*Jah.* For sure and for certain."

"So this means that Peter didn't legally adopt me until I was older," William said.

"My guess would be that it took a while for your biological father to agree to sign the papers. Perhaps he didn't want to give you up." Uncle George raised a brow. "I tried not to be too involved in their lives, especially after what happened with Christopher. I didn't know all the details, but, although Peter treated you like a son, you probably weren't *officially* adopted until later. I wouldn't be surprised if Peter finally paid Elam a little visit, and insisted he relinquish his parental rights so he could adopt you and you could have a proper father."

Will shrugged. "Well, unless we find more journal notes or letters, I guess we'll never know. But, now, I'm glad he did."

He smiled at Sally, then grasped her hand and brought it to his lips.

Ding dong.

"I wonder who that could be." Will looked to Saloma.

George shot up. "That, William, would be for me. I have a date." He winked.

"You, Uncle George? A date?"

He chuckled. "Don't sound so surprised. I still have a few good years left in me."

"Who is it?"

"Remember Ms. Johnson?"

"The young widow from church?"

"That's the one." Uncle George's eyes sparkled. "Well, I've gotta go. Don't want to keep my date waiting."

Will watched in amazement as his uncle flounced through the door.

His gazed moved to Sally. "Well, I guess it's just us now."

"*Jah.*"

Will drew Sally into his arms and held her the way he'd been longing to. His lips met hers once, then he pulled away. "Guess what, Sally."

"What?" Her beautiful knowing smile melted his heart once again.

His lips met hers. "I'm not your brother."

Sally bit her bottom lip. "I know."

"Sally?"

"Yes, Will?"

"I love you more than anything in this world." He pushed a stray strand of hair back behind her ear. "Will you marry me?"

Her eyes portrayed surprise, but he knew she half expected it. "Now?"

"I wish." He lightly caressed her cheek. "As soon as possible?"

"*Jah*, Will. I would love to marry you."

He drew her close again. "Sally?"

"Yes, Will?"

"I think I'd better take you home," he said breathily, forcing himself away.

Saloma laughed. "*Jah.* I think you're right."

He sobered. "Let's pray, first."

"*Jah.* That is a *wunderbaar* idea."

William took Saloma's hands in his, and they both bowed their heads in prayer, giving thanks to their Heavenly Father above for His blessed provision.

THIRTY-THREE

"Are you ready to go, Sally?" Will called from the great room. Sally wanted to freshen up before they attended the evening candlelight service.

"Coming." She appeared from the hallway. "Will your uncle be there too?"

"I'm guessing he will." Will smiled. "I'm glad your mother is letting you come with me."

"I think she was overjoyed when you gave her back the money she paid for the lease and told her about the house." Saloma grinned. "That, and our supper plans with the Yoders were cancelled because one of their *kinner* is sick."

"Bad for them, good for me. It's unfortunate they're not feeling well on Christmas Eve, though. That's a bummer." He snatched the keys from his pocket and held out his elbow. "My lady."

Sally smiled and hooked her arm into the crook of Will's elbow and they walked out to his Jeep. He opened the door and assisted Sally's entrance.

"I'm going to talk to the pastor tonight," Will informed her.

"About us?"

"Yeah. How soon do you think he'll be able to perform our ceremony?"

Sally shrugged. She seemed unusually quiet.

Will observed her pensiveness. "What are you thinking about?"

"My birth mother."

Will's brow rose. "Your birth mother?"

"Will, if my birth mother is still alive then I'd like to meet her."

"Why?"

"Think about it. If she hadn't given me up, who knows where I would have grown up? Who knows what kind of a terrible life I might have had? If she hadn't given me up, then you and I would have probably never met."

His eyes widened. "You're right." He leaned over and met her lips. "I think I'd like to give her a hug myself."

Sally laughed. "You'd better keep your eyes on the road."

"Hey, Pastor Rob, that was a great service." Will shook the pastor's hand.

"Thank you, William. God's wonders never cease."

"Isn't that the truth! As a matter of fact, Sally and I were wondering when you'd be able to marry us." He winked at Sally, then turned back to Pastor Rob.

"We require at least six weeks of marriage counseling."

Will winced. He'd forgotten all about counseling. He internally laughed at himself. *A counselor forgetting about counseling.*

"Any time after that would be fine." The pastor looked at both Sally and Will. "Congratulations."

"*Denki.*" Will loved seeing Sally's glow.

"Thank you, Pastor." Will smiled. "Merry Christmas."

"I'm curious about something, William." Pastor Rob raised a brow. "How did you and your fiancé overcome your obstacles? I thought you were siblings."

William nodded. "So did we. Let's just say it took a lot of prayer and a miracle. I'd thought it was impossible. It sure seemed like it. But apparently, it was just a trial."

Pastor Rob agreed. "God sometimes allows us to go through trials so that we learn to trust in Him. If we learn our lesson, our faith will come out stronger, and we'll be able to face the next trial with greater confidence."

EPILOGUE

Six months later...

Saloma gazed at her handsome husband and smiled.

"Are you ready?" Will reached over the seat and grasped her hand.

Sally looked out the tiny window next to her seat. "Are you sure and certain this airplane will stay in the air?"

Will chuckled. "Yes. Unless God calls us home."

"I wonder what Hawaii will be like." She'd seen the pictures in the brochures, but everything always seemed better in person.

"I'm sure it will be beautiful. Just like my gorgeous wife." He leaned over and kissed her on the lips, not caring who was watching. "We'll have the best honeymoon ever. You can count on that."

"Your uncle was kind to give us this gift."

"Oh, yeah! He said he had something else for us too." Will stood up and took one of their carry-on bags out of the upper luggage compartment. He pulled out an envelope and handed it to Sally. "Here. He said for us to open this on our honeymoon. I think now qualifies."

Saloma opened the envelope, much like the one Will's uncle had given them at Christmas, only this one was white. She pulled out a card and read the words, "Dear William and Saloma, I hope you two are having the time of your lives. By the time you read this, my beautiful Ms. Magdalena Johnson and I will be married as well. I know this may be a shock, but this is the way we wanted it to be. I have another surprise. I have purchased a second home in North Carolina where Magdalena and I will reside, but, rest assured, we will visit often. I've deeded the home in Pennsylvania to you, William. I was going to put it into my will, but I figured I might as well give it to you now. Please come visit us this summer at our oceanfront cottage. We look forward to seeing you. Have a wonderful honeymoon; I know we will! Love, Uncle George and Aunt Magdalena Anderson."

William sat open-mouthed. "Wow! I can't believe that. Who knew?"

Sally's eyes widened. "We have a house?"

"Yes, Sally. Our very own house."

Her face brightened. "With plenty of room for lots of *bopplin!*"

Will's lips met Sally's. "Yes, my beautiful wife. We'll be getting started on those real soon."

Saloma sighed contently and held tight to Will's hand as the airplane began traveling at a faster pace. They'd already been instructed to fasten their seatbelts. She watched out the window as the plane lifted into the air and eventually soared in the sky, the objects on the ground becoming smaller and smaller until she could see only clouds beneath them.

She briefly bowed her head and again gave thanks to the Father above for His wonderful provision. Indeed, God was good. Even when everything in life seemed impossible, God was good.

A SPECIAL THANK YOU

*To our fabulous **Street Team**, who help us 'Sprede the Word'*

*To our **Proofing Team**, you know who you are* ☺

*To **Kim**, our awesome editor*

*To **Heather**, our gifted paperback formatter
at Art & Design Studios*

*To **Lucinda**, our talented Smashwords formatter*

*To **Brandi**, the best VA ever*

*And, of course, to our **Lord and Saviour,
Jesus Christ** – our reason for writing*

Other offerings from Blessed Publishing:

MICHELYNN CHRISTY

A Short
Love Story

A
Christmas
to Remember

A *Christmas* to Remember

MICHELYNN CHRISTY

Determined not to spend Christmas alone, Samantha reluctantly returns home for the holidays. She'd escaped her hometown by running off to college over a year ago, nursing a broken heart. But now that she's returned, she must face her regrets head on. Will she be able to find joy - and possibly love - this holiday season? A novelette. Contemporary Christian Romance

E-book Only $0.99 at Amazon.com

CPSIA information can be obtained
at www.ICGtesting.com
Printed in the USA
BVOW03s0223240217
476870BV00003B/352/P